"How about a quickie while we're eighteen floors up?"

Teddy gasped as Austin stopped the elevator. "You're outrageous!"

Austin raised his eyebrow. "You have to admit that the thought is thrilling...maybe just a little bit."

He glanced down. It would be just a matter of lifting her dress, removing her panties, unzipping his pants and letting her sit on that sturdy brass bar behind them as she wrapped her legs around his hips....

He nearly groaned at the erotic image. Running his fingers down her body, he whispered, "What do you say, Teddy?"

Teddy shivered. Then, lifting her hand, she sifted her fingers through the hair at the nape of his neck and brought his mouth down to hers. "Yes," she murmured, giving him a deep kiss more powerful than any aphrodisiac.

Passion rose quickly to the surface, shattering his control. He had to have her. But just as his palm touched her silken thigh, a shrill ring filled the small cubicle. Through the fog of desire, Austin realized it was the emergency phone.

He picked up the receiver. "No, there's no trouble." Then, hanging up the phone, he set the elevator in motion again and turned to Teddy. "We still have a long way to go," he said with a wicked grin. "Where were we?"

Dear Reader,

If you could ask Santa to leave the man of your dreams under your tree, what would he be? A rugged construction worker? A dashing man in uniform? A dapper executive? The possibilities are endless—and very intriguing! Teddy Spencer has always fantasized about a sexy-as-sin cowboy, who'd lasso her heart and then ride off into the sunset with her. But she'd never dreamed she'd ever meet her fantasy man in the flesh— or have the right to call him hers indefinitely!

Austin McBride is in the business of fulfilling women's fantasies. However, he isn't in the habit of personally offering his services to damsels in distress, until sexy Teddy Spencer's proposition makes him decide to give himself an early Christmas gift. Teddy needs a lover…and Austin is just the man for the job!

Christmas Fantasy is the first book in the FANTASY FOR HIRE miniseries. In the spin-off book, Austin's brother Jordan gets a little too close for comfort with an irrepressible—and irresistible—reporter. Don't miss *Valentine Fantasy* by Jamie Denton, available in January 2000.

Happy holidays!

Janelle Denison

P.S. I'd love to know what you thought of *Christmas Fantasy*. You can write to me at P.O. Box 1102, Rialto, CA 92377-1102. I look forward to hearing from you!

Books by Janelle Denison

HARLEQUIN TEMPTATION
679—PRIVATE PLEASURES
682—PRIVATE FANTASIES
732—FORBIDDEN

CHRISTMAS FANTASY
Janelle Denison

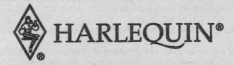

TORONTO • NEW YORK • LONDON
AMSTERDAM • PARIS • SYDNEY • HAMBURG
STOCKHOLM • ATHENS • TOKYO • MILAN • MADRID
PRAGUE • WARSAW • BUDAPEST • AUCKLAND

To Laura Novak and Barb Hoeter, two very special
people who make what I do so pleasurable and fulfilling.

And, as always, to Don,
for showing me that reality can be
so much richer than fantasy.

ISBN 0-373-25859-3

CHRISTMAS FANTASY

Copyright © 1999 by Janelle Denison.

Visit us at www.romance.net

Printed in U.S.A.

1

TEDDY SPENCER'S two good friends, Brenda and Laura, could always be counted on for a good time, especially when it came to marking a special occasion. It was the perfect excuse for them to get wild and crazy, and although Teddy considered herself the more reserved of the trio, after a few mai tai's that feisty, rebellious side of her personality—the one her parents hadn't been able to tame—usually made an appearance.

After spending the past hour and a half at a subdued birthday dinner with her parents at the local country club, and listening once again to her parents' favorite speech lately—that she was getting older and needed to settle down like the rest of her siblings had—Teddy welcomed the opportunity to let loose with her friends. She was on her second mai tai, and thoroughly enjoying herself, even if Brenda had embarrassed her by swiping the deejay's microphone and announcing to everyone in the Frisco Bay Bar that it was Teddy's twenty-sixth birthday. Teddy had thought that fairly obvious by the half-dozen balloons attached to her chair and the I'm-the-birthday-girl pennant Brenda and Laura had insisted she wear, but Brenda had a way of coaxing everyone to join in on the fun.

If that hadn't been embarrassing enough, having fifty pairs of eyes watch her open presents from Brenda and Laura brought a warm flush to her cheeks. The gifts had included an array of skimpy lingerie, not to mention other sensual delights. The single men in the room had issued wolf whistles, and Teddy found herself overwhelmed by invitations to model the silky, provocative underwear.

The bartender delivered the chocolate cake Laura had smuggled to him earlier and, as Brenda lit the single "26" candle, the deejay played "Happy Birthday." Everyone in the lounge chorused the traditional song just for her.

It was all in good fun, and just what Teddy needed to take a break from the stress she was under at work, and make her forget about her parents' quest to diminish the independence she'd worked so hard to gain over the past few years. She knew her mother and father meant well. Unfortunately, their views of what was important to her, and for her, varied drastically from her own.

Determined to enjoy the evening, she pushed aside those troubling thoughts. As the lounge settled back to its normal din, and she was able to relax without being the center of attention, Teddy shook her head at her friends. "You two are outrageous."

As if Teddy had just issued a compliment, a grin brightened Laura's classical features. "Yeah, we are outrageous, aren't we?"

"And damn proud of it, too," Brenda added, her eyes dancing with mischief. "Heck, there's no telling what we might do next."

Teddy lifted an eyebrow at the insinuation in Brenda's voice, but her friend merely feigned innocence. Suspecting something was up, but unable to guess how they could possibly top the evening so far, she glanced at her cake...and frowned at the inscription they'd chosen.

"Happy birthday and congratulations?" She looked from one friend to the other.

Brenda nodded. "We're combining your birthday and your senior graphic design promotion all together."

Teddy smiled, genuinely touched. "That's sweet of you, but I haven't gotten the promotion yet." Whether she did or not wouldn't be decided for another two and a half weeks, just after the new year.

Laura gave Teddy's knee an encouraging pat. "See how much faith we have in you?"

Teddy wished she had that much faith in herself. It wasn't that she wasn't qualified for the job—she'd double majored in graphic design and had a master's degree in business administration, not to mention being an exemplary employee. It was her boss, Louden Avery, who was making her advancement within Sharper Image Advertising so difficult.

"Come on, Teddy." Brenda nudged her with her elbow. "Blow out your candle and make a wish."

Teddy absently toyed with the ruby and diamond band on her left-hand ring finger. It bothered her that she felt forced to wear a ring to discourage Louden's subtle interest in her, and back up the claim that she had a steady boyfriend. But it was the only thing she could think of. Taking a deep breath, she blew out the single flame and hopefully secured her future. Her wish was simple. She wanted that promotion, awarded to her on her own merit.

"Wow," Brenda breathed dreamily. "If I had to make a wish, he would be it."

Teddy followed her friend's line of vision to the entrance of the Frisco Bay, and caught her breath at the sight of a gorgeous hunk making his way through the Tuesday-evening crowd. Every woman in the establishment was staring at him—for two very good reasons. One, his mere presence was captivating, and two, his unusual attire stood out conspicuously against all the power suits filling the trendy bar. He was the epitome of a cowboy, from the beige Stetson on his head, to the pearl-snap western shirt covering a wide chest, to the chaps and worn jeans that molded to trim hips and muscular thighs, all the way down to his scuffed leather boots. He looked as if he'd just stepped out of the Wild West, though he didn't appear to be uncomfortable in the ultra-urban setting, surrounded by a crowd of Ivy League patrons.

He sidled up to a vacant spot in front of the bar and ordered a drink. While he waited for the bartender to return, he scanned the people in the lounge as if searching for someone. Annoyingly enough, the brim of his Stetson cast shadows over the upper portion of his face, but Teddy caught a glimpse of chiseled features, a well-defined mouth and dark brown hair that curled over his collar at the nape of his neck.

He turned his head her way. Even though she couldn't see his eyes because of that damn hat, she got the distinct impression he was looking directly at her. The corner of his mouth kicked up ever so slightly in an I've-got-you-now kind of smile. Her skin warmed and tightened, and something deep within Teddy fluttered with awareness. It was a sensation unlike anything she'd ever experienced.

She forced her gaze from him and drew a stabilizing breath. "Wow is right," she murmured in agreement, and was a little surprised that she'd spoken her thoughts out loud.

Laura issued a reciprocating sound of appreciation and turned to look at Teddy. A sassy grin curved her lips. "What do you think, birthday girl? Would you like to take a ride with that cowboy?"

Laura's question made all kinds of images spring into Teddy's mind. She thought of leather, the scent of hay, the jangling sounds of spurs and the fun she'd have if he'd let her ride... Suddenly, what he stood for had become more erotic than she cared to admit.

"He's kind of out of place, don't you think?" she said nonchalantly, trying to keep her friends, the bloodhounds that they were, at bay. "San Francisco isn't known for its ranches. Maybe he's lost."

"Maybe he's looking for a good time." Brenda wiggled her eyebrows lasciviously. "I'm sure it gets awfully lonely out on the range."

As casually as possible, Teddy slid her gaze back to the cowboy, hoping he'd moved on to peruse another woman, considering any one of the ladies in the lounge would have killed for a smidgen of his attention. But no, he was still staring at her, and as she watched, he tipped his Stetson, then reached beside him for the glass that the bartender had delivered. He saluted her, and took a long drink of the dark liquid that looked like whiskey.

Her own mouth went dry, and she reached for her mai tai. The cool, sweet-tangy mixture did little to extinguish the heat spreading through her.

"Didn't you once say you wanted a cowboy of your own, Teddy?" Brenda asked.

Teddy was startled that Brenda remembered that crazy night nearly six months ago when they'd sat at this very table and spun fantasies about the men in the lounge— imagining who they could be beneath their Armani suits and executive image. At the time, Teddy had wanted a cowboy, because it bucked convention—or rather her parents' stuffy standards.

"We were just fooling around, and I think I had one too many mai tais." Setting her drink back on the table, Teddy waved a hand in the air. "It was just a fantasy, Brenda."

Laura leaned toward Teddy, a meaningful glimmer in

her eyes. "Well, honey, fantasy is about to become reality."

Suspicion twisted through Teddy as her two friends exchanged a covert look. "What are you guys up to?"

"Hey, cowboy," Brenda called out. "We've got a birthday girl over here who has a thing for cowboys. Do you think you could oblige her?"

Teddy's jaw dropped, and her face heated in mortification. Before she could recover from her shock, her fantasy man moved away from the bar and strolled lazily toward them.

"I'll certainly do my best," he drawled in a deep, rich voice that carried across the room and snagged a good amount of attention. The women he passed looked on with envy and longing, not that her cowboy noticed. His gaze was trained on her, and the smile curving his mouth was pure, unadulterated sin.

Closer and closer he came. Teddy's heart tripled its beat, and a mixture of excitement and apprehension warred within her. "Are you nuts?" she whispered to Brenda.

"Naw." Brenda winked at Teddy. "Laura and I wanted to do something special for your birthday. He's all yours, at least for the next twenty minutes."

Teddy blinked. "I don't understand..."

Laura gave her a jaunty grin. "It's all very simple. Just enjoy yourself, and the fantasy."

Teddy wanted a better explanation than that, but there wasn't time to ask. Her fantasy was standing beside her chair. Hesitantly, she glanced his way, and found herself eye level with a pair of sinewy thighs wrapped in soft leather chaps that molded to his lean hips and strong legs, and profiled what made him impressively male. She forced her gaze higher, taking in a body honed to masculine perfection—virile, sexy and scrumptious enough to send her pulse racing.

It was a long climb up—she estimated his height well over six foot—but the trek was extremely enjoyable. By the time she reached her cowboy's face and saw the warm, private smile flirting with the corners of his mouth, she felt breathless.

And then she saw his eyes for the first time. They were a striking green, with gold flecks that mesmerized and seduced. He had ridiculously long, dark lashes, and she had the fleeting thought that his eyes alone could tempt a woman to shed her inhibitions, and anything else he might request.

He touched his long fingers to the brim of his Stetson in a brief caress that had her thinking about those hands of his, and how they'd feel against her skin. It was a maddening, and totally inappropriate, thought, considering she didn't know him at all, but if this was her fantasy, she intended to enjoy it to its fullest.

"Care to dance, darlin'?" he asked, the perfect gentleman.

She melted just a little, and speech suddenly became a difficult task. "I, uh..."

Brenda lifted Teddy's hand toward the cowboy and winked at him. "She'd love to dance, and anything else you might be inspired to do."

"It would be my pleasure," he murmured huskily.

Uneasiness rippled down Teddy's spine, putting her feminine senses on alert. What would be his pleasure? she wondered, feeling as though she was in the middle of a conspiracy.

What were Brenda and Laura up to?

A warm hand clasped hers, pulled her to her feet, and she found herself being led to the dance floor, which was currently vacant. That didn't seem to bother her partner, who gave the deejay a brief nod. As if on cue, the young man put on a slow, country ballad and announced into his microphone, "This one is for you, Teddy."

If that dedication wasn't perplexing enough, the soft, crooning voice drifting from the speakers totally bewildered her. In all the times she'd come to the Frisco Bay in the past two years, not once had she ever heard a country song. The deejay played rock and roll, and on occasion, a slow tune by a popular soft-rock artist. If you wanted country music, you went to the Silver Spur.

The plot was getting thicker and thicker...

Like a man accustomed to taking the lead, her cowboy smoothly pulled her against him, aligning their bodies intimately. One arm slipped around her lower back, keeping her from attempting to put any distance between them, and his other hand held hers loosely to the side. Very hesitantly, because she really had no choice, she lightly rested her free hand on his biceps...nice, strong, muscular biceps.

She kept her gaze averted, focusing on the crowd of onlookers over his shoulder, while valiantly trying to distract her body's response to the man who held her so provocatively.

It was no use. Through the silk of her blouse and the cotton of his shirt, she experienced the crush of his hard chest against her soft breasts that had suddenly become achingly sensitive. And there was certainly no way she could dismiss the subtle pressure of his belly against hers, or the arousing friction of his leather chaps scraping against her thighs where the hem of her skirt ended. It was like being charged head to toe with an electrical shock.

She'd danced with plenty of men through the years, but

none had ever ignited such an instantaneous blaze of heat, or made her so aware of herself as a woman.

It was thrilling, incredibly sexy and unnerving.

As he moved her in a circle on the dance floor, she caught sight of her friends. Brenda grinned and gave her a thumbs-up, and Laura snapped a picture of her and the cowboy.

Cringing at their enthusiasm, she cast a surreptitious glance at the man she was dancing with, only to find him staring at her, his eyes taking on a smoky moss hue. She felt the stroke of his thumb along her spine, the press of his large palm against the small of her back, and shivered. His warm breath fluttered a silky strand of hair near her cheek, and she caught an odd scent. She'd expected to inhale the strong odor of whiskey from his drink. Instead, she encountered the delectable fragrance of root beer, which made something curl deep within her. The man drank root beer, of all things! Briefly, she wondered if he tasted as sweet and warm as he smelled.

Clearing her suddenly dry throat, she pushed the forbidden thoughts aside and forced herself to break the silence between them. "This is, um, incredibly awkward. My friends can be a bit wild, and I'm sure they put you on the spot." She licked her bottom lip nervously. "Dancing with me really isn't necessary."

He blinked lazily, a slow sweep of those gorgeous lashes. "Darlin', I find it hard to refuse a woman's fantasy, especially on her birthday."

She detected an underlying insinuation to his words, but wasn't quite sure what he meant by that cryptic remark. She wasn't quite sure she wanted to know, either. Deciding to make the best of the two minutes left to the song, she introduced herself. "I'm Teddy Spencer."

There was a bit of mischief in his eyes, as if he knew a

secret and she didn't. "Austin McBride," he offered. "And it's a pleasure to meet you, Teddy."

There was that word again, *pleasure*. This time, though, the way he rolled it together so seductively with her name caused a flurry of sensations to erupt within her. It tickled her belly and spread out toward her thighs and breasts. Her reaction was crazy, confusing and exhilarating in a very unladylike way.

You're shameless, Teddy, her good-girl consciousness taunted. The wicked, bad-girl part of her was beginning not to care.

She gave him an upswept look, along with a flirtatious smile she hadn't used in what seemed like years. There was an undeniable chemistry between them, though reserved on his part, and it made her feel daring, and a little reckless.

She slid her hand up his arm, until her fingers touched the soft strands of hair lying against the collar of his shirt. She had the sudden urge to take off that Stetson of his so she could see his face. But knowing how inappropriate that would be, she held herself back.

"So, Mr. McBride," she said, surprising herself with the throaty quality of her voice. "Are you really a cowboy?"

"As real as it gets in San Francisco, I suppose." He followed that up with a private, playful wink.

She lifted an eyebrow, intent on finding out more about this mysterious man. "I take it you're not from around here, then?"

He expertly moved her to the slow beat of the music, dancing with her as if they were the only two in the bar. "As a matter of fact, I am."

She regarded him with a combination of curiosity and speculation. "I wasn't aware of any ranches in the area."

The corner of his generous mouth quirked, but he

didn't comment. "So, it's your birthday, hmm?" he asked, smoothly changing the subject.

She rolled her eyes. "Trussed up like I am with this silly pennant, it's kind of difficult *not* to know it's my birthday."

He smiled, his eyes shimmering with warmth and a scampish spark. "Well, your friends got you a very special present."

At that moment the song they were swaying to ended, and before she could take in what he'd said, or politely excuse herself from his wonderfully solid body, he maneuvered her four large steps back, until the curve of her knees hit a lounge chair someone had put out on the dance floor. Wide-eyed, she tumbled into the cushioned seat. Startled on more levels than one, she frantically sought out her two friends.

She found them, but quickly realized neither one would be any source of help. Both Brenda and Laura wore goofy grins. Laura lifted her camera, and a bright flash momentarily blinded Teddy, but she had no problem hearing Brenda yell, "Take if off for her, cowboy!"

A flush of mortification burned Teddy's cheeks as she realized she'd been set up. New music blared out of the speakers, an upbeat, rock-a-billy tune that encouraged her cowboy to move his hips in such a provocative fashion, it took her breath away.

Belatedly, she realized his intent and attempted to escape while there was still a chance. "I really don't think—"

He leaned forward and braced his arms on either side of her chair, crowding her between hunter-green tweed and an unyielding wall of masculinity. "No, don't think at all," he agreed in a teasing drawl. "Just sit back, relax and enjoy your fantasy, darlin'." Lifting his hand, he withdrew the beige Stetson from his head and settled it lightly on the crown of hers. "And here's a little something to remember me by."

Oh, God. Backdropped by thick, luxurious, dark brown hair, his eyes seemed greener, sexier, if that were even possible. But her muddled mind only had a handful of seconds to register that fact before he straightened, ending her hypnotic state of fascination.

Then he stepped back, and while his hips moved rhythmically to the beat of the music, he grasped the sides of his western shirt and ripped open the pearl snaps securing the front. Teddy gasped, and the women in the Frisco Bay went wild—of which Brenda and Laura were the loudest and most unrestrained in their cheering. The men in the establishment looked on with idle amusement.

Despite a fond wish to be anywhere but sitting in the middle of the dance floor with a gorgeous man stripping for her, she found herself totally mesmerized by Austin McBride. Fascinated by his eat-'em-up eyes. Stunned by his breathtaking smile. Enthralled by his incredible body.

It had been a long time since a man had captured her interest so thoroughly.

With a wicked grin, he turned around and slowly shrugged out of his shirt, letting the cotton fabric slide down his arms to reveal a smooth, powerful-looking back that sloped to a trim waist. There wasn't an ounce of fat on her cowboy that she could tell—even that nice, cute butt of his was all firm muscle as he gave it an enticing wriggle that had the women screaming for more.

Yanking the shirt from the waistband of his faded jeans, he tossed the garment over his shoulder, and it landed right in the middle of her lap. The material was warm against her stocking-clad thighs, and smelled earthy and male. She had little time to register that before he tugged on the sides of his chaps and the Velcro holding them on gave way. Those, too, came sailing her way, the soft leather draping across her legs like a lover's caress.

Though the low-slung jeans he wore had a well-worn look about them, they were snug enough to mold to his narrow hips and the long, muscular length of his thighs and legs. The soft-looking material was creased and faded in all the right places, and even a little threadbare in the most intriguing spots, she noticed, as he slowly, sensuously, rolled his hips to the tempo of the music.

His long fingers settled on the heavy belt buckle cinching his waist, and Teddy's stomach bottomed out. But she couldn't look away. With a lazy flick of his wrist, the leather strap slipped from the buckle, the movement slow and somehow erotic. Leaving the belt on and hanging open, he moved close enough for her to reach out and touch the tight muscles rippling along his belly. The dare in his eyes was unmistakable—he expected *her* to take off his belt!

Someone in the crowd let out a shrill, wolf whistle, followed up with, "Go for it!"

Austin grinned, obviously used to such enthusiastic displays. "You heard the lady," he drawled encouragingly. "Go for it."

And so Teddy did. Grasping the metal buckle, she gave it a tentative tug. Austin gyrated his hips at the same moment, and the belt slid from the loopholes on his jeans and into her hands. The strip of leather was warm and supple against her palm, inciting naughty thoughts that shocked even herself. She groaned at her runaway imagination, grateful that no one could hear her over the noise in the bar. The music pulsated, the beat seemingly as raw and primitive as the man before her.

She expected him to strip off his jeans like most male

exotic dancers did, but he made no attempt to remove that last barrier of clothing. Instead, he danced for her wearing nothing but his formfitting jeans and a sinfully wicked smile. But, oh, this provocative teasing was so much more arousing than watching him strip down to a skimpy G-string, which would have spoiled the illusion he'd created. This teasing glimpse gave her enough to stir her imagination and incite future cowboy fantasies.

It was apparent Austin McBride knew exactly how to stimulate a woman's senses, and he used that knowledge to his advantage. He rocked his honed body to the beat of the music, giving her time to take in his bare chest, dusted with a light sprinkling of dark brown hair. Unable to help herself, she followed that trail down to where it whorled around his navel, then disappeared into the waistband of his jeans. And when he turned, giving her a view of his backside, the muscles across his shoulders bunched, and his tight bottom and sinewy thighs flexed with the easy, rhythmic movement of his body.

He was truly a work of art.

She licked her dry lips, suddenly feeling as though someone in the establishment had kicked up the temperature ten degrees. Her face was warm—hell, her entire body was prickly with fever—and her breathing was deep and labored.

When her gaze lifted back to his face, his eyes were filled with a combination of sultry heat, immense charm and forbidden enticement. It was all a well-orchestrated act. She knew that, so why did she experience such an inexplicable connection between them, one that went beyond immediate sexual attraction to something deeper and mystifying in that man-woman way?

Not soon enough to suit her embarrassment, the music ended and her fantasy was over. She glanced over at

Brenda and Laura and narrowed her gaze. Brenda grinned outrageously and blew at the tip of her finger as if it were the smoking end of a gun—*too hot* was her unmistakable message—and Laura waggled her fingers at Teddy impishly.

No doubt about it, Teddy was going to kill her two best friends.

AUSTIN MCBRIDE INWARDLY cringed as the Frisco Bay broke into a roar of raucous cheers, whistles and applause, and tried not to let his growing discomfort show. It was an odd sensation to find himself uncomfortable in what should have been a very familiar, and routine, situation.

However, three months ago, at the age of thirty, while standing center stage wearing nothing more than a tight pair of pants with a roomful of women going crazy with lust, Austin had come to the conclusion that he was getting too old, and certainly less assertive and brazen, to be taking his clothes off in public. As owner and founder of Fantasy for Hire, he'd made the decision to retire his outrageous costumes, and let his younger and more energetic employees handle the exotic, and sometimes outrageous, fantasies women requested.

Tonight had been the exception. Taking off his clothes had been a necessity, not a choice. Don, one of his most requested strippers, had called Austin on his cell phone to tell him that someone had sideswiped his car, and although he was physically okay, he wouldn't be able to make his seven o'clock appointment at the Frisco Bay. That gave Austin a little over an hour to scramble to find someone to fill in. The two guys he managed to get hold of didn't have the requested cowboy costume on hand—but Austin did. Deciding it would be simpler to take care of the engagement himself since time was so limited, he'd donned his western attire, all the while swearing this would be the very last time he fulfilled a woman's fantasy outside of a bedroom.

Tonight's incident only served to shore up his decision to put Fantasy for Hire on the market for a new owner. In the past six years his shoot-from-the-hip venture had increased beyond his wildest expectations, expanding from two part-time employees to nearly a dozen young men who were willing to fulfill a woman's twenty-minute fantasy for ample compensation.

Austin had been amazed by the popularity of his business. Fulfilling fantasies, it seemed, was a very profitable commodity. Fantasy for Hire was so inundated with requests that he was turning away more customers than he had fantasies available.

Despite the fact that the business cut into too much of his personal life of late, it was hard to complain about Fantasy's success. The company had served its purpose in supplementing his income to help pay for the school loans and bills he'd accumulated while embarking on another venture in commercial landscaping nearly four years ago.

His second business and ultimate career choice, McBride Commercial Landscaping, was finally lucrative and self-sufficient. Now, Austin wanted a life. One that didn't include costumes and games, or bringing fantasies to life for hundreds of faceless women who clung to the illusions he displayed. He'd discovered the hard way that women found it difficult to separate him from the part he played. Once he performed for a customer, he couldn't be sure if she wanted him for himself, or the private fantasy he'd created for her.

That's why he'd established his own personal rule a few years ago, after being used for one woman's particular fantasy. The customers he performed for were off limits, no matter how intriguing the woman. And he found Teddy Spencer plenty fascinating, from the sleek cut of her silky blond hair that brushed her shoulders with a slight undercurl, to her big brown eyes that combined wholesomeness with a heady dose of sensuality, to those shapely killer legs extending from the hem of her short, teal-colored business suit. Her cream-hued blouse was pure silk, and although it was buttoned primly enough, he could see the faintest outline of lace shaping her full breasts. She was a dynamite package of sophistication and casual elegance, a distinct kind of demeanor shaped by old money and ingrained from birth. Those obvious signs should have warned him off, but the awareness that had leaped to life between them while they'd danced was still too fresh in his mind.

Once the noise in the bar lessened, she lifted his shirt toward him with a wavering smile on her lips and the color of roses staining her smooth cheeks. "I, um, guess you'd like your clothes back?"

Her tentative question made him smile. The way she so easily blushed was refreshing—an endearing, old-fashioned quality he didn't see very often these days. "It is getting a little drafty in here." He took his shirt from her, and slipped into it. He didn't bother to snap the front closed—it was a little late to worry about a "no shirt, no service" policy.

Grasping her hand, he helped her to her feet. The touch was simple, an everyday, gentlemanly gesture, but when his fingers slid against her soft palm he heard her breath catch and saw something in her eyes flare. Incredibly, his body flashed a reciprocating heat that spiraled low in his belly.

For the first time in years, Austin thought about mixing

business with pleasure, until he saw the ruby and diamond ring staking a claim on her left hand. A woman didn't wear a sparkly ring on that finger unless she was taken.

It was too bad, but just as well—considering the only thing he had in common with her fantasy cowboy was his love of outdoors. Take off all the western trappings, and he was just a simple, hardworking, blue-collar city man. Hardly a match for her.

"You were a great sport," he said, distracting himself from the attraction racing between them.

She groaned, the sound rife with chagrin. "As if I had a choice." She shot her two friends an I'm-going-to-get-you-for-this kind of look.

He grinned. "Happy birthday, Teddy." Lifting her hand to his mouth, he brushed his lips over the back of her knuckles. A fleeting touch as soft as a butterfly's wing. The gallant kiss wasn't a service he normally provided for his customers, but he couldn't stop the urge to give her one last thing to remember this evening by. "It really *was* my pleasure."

He let her go, leaving her speechless, and gathered up the rest of his things. He'd taken two steps off the dance floor when she exclaimed, "Oh, your hat!"

He turned back around, and because she'd closed the distance between them, he tipped back the Stetson on her head with a flick of his finger. "I meant it when I said it was yours to keep. Compliments of Fantasy for Hire, and your girlfriends." He gave her one last wink. "It's up to you to explain to your boyfriend where you got it."

She appeared startled by his last comment, but he didn't give her time to respond. The gig was up. No more pretenses. Back to real life.

He headed toward the entrance of the Frisco Bay, and he didn't look back.

He never did.

2

SHE COULDN'T STOP thinking about him.

Teddy leaned back in her office chair and flicked her finger along the corner of the white business card that stated simply, Compliments Of Fantasy for Hire. With a soft sigh, she stroked her thumb over the bold, black raised letters of Austin McBride's name embossed on the left-hand corner. Beneath that was the business phone number, which was permanently etched in her mind.

She'd found the rectangular card as she'd set the Stetson on her bedroom dresser when she'd gotten home last night after her impromptu birthday bash. It had been tucked into the thin leather band around the crown, and since Laura and Brenda had insisted she wear the hat the entire evening, she hadn't discovered it until later.

The card certainly wasn't an invitation to call, not unless she wanted a repeat performance from Austin, which she didn't. She recognized the business card for the piece of advertisement it was—referrals and word of mouth went a long way in making a business successful—so why had she slipped the card into her purse this morning instead of leaving it at home with her birthday Stetson?

She couldn't stop thinking about him.

It was a pitiful excuse, but there it was. She reminded herself that she couldn't afford a distraction like Austin McBride, fantasy extraordinaire, not when she was so close to achieving the goals she'd set for herself. Goals that included a solid, steady career and complete independence from the overbearing family that still hadn't recovered from the shock that she'd broken off her engagement to the affluent Bartholomew Winston two years ago. Her plans didn't include a man, especially one who fulfilled women's fantasies on a regular basis.

She had to stop thinking about him. That's all there was to it, she decided. Opening the middle drawer of her oak desk, she set the card on top of the other business cards stacked neatly in a small partition in the left-hand corner.

"Out of sight, out of mind," she muttered, doubting those six words would be able to make her forget her gorgeous, green-eyed cowboy.

"Is that problem with your sight and mind going to affect your performance on the World Wide Travel account?"

Startled by the intrusion, Teddy pinched the tip of her index finger in her desk drawer just as it closed. Wincing, she glanced up and gave the man approaching her desk a barely tolerable look. Louden Avery, her boss and creative director at Sharper Image, considered himself above the courtesy of knocking or announcing his presence.

He strolled into her office as if he owned it, his pale blue eyes missing nothing, not the remnants of a half-eaten lunch that attested to the extra hour she'd worked without compensation, or the files and sketches on her desk that she was currently devoting time to, or even what she wore. The latter was the worst, because he took his time about it. By the time he finished his deliberate perusal, her jaw ached from gritting her teeth.

Keeping in mind that he was her boss, she summoned a pleasant smile she was certain didn't quite reach her eyes. "Contrary to what you might have heard, my sight and mind are sound."

"That's good to know," he replied with calculated mildness. "I wouldn't want anything to impair your chances of getting that promotion."

"The only thing that could hurt my chances is if someone more qualified than myself come along." After all, they both knew she had the experience, along with a degree that gave her a distinct advantage over Fred Williams, the colleague she was up against.

Louden merely smiled. Rounding her desk, he propped his hip on the corner nearest her, unmindful of the papers resting on the edge. Bracing his left forearm on his thigh, he leaned toward her, though his gaze was busy taking in the project laid out in front of her. "How is the preliminary sketch coming on the World Wide Travel logo?"

"Just fine." Louden liked to feel superior, and she had no doubt that his position on her desk had been chosen for such a purpose. She forced herself to look up at him, determined to meet his gaze. "It'll be on your desk first thing in the morning, two days before deadline."

"My, aren't you efficient." Using a slim finger, he turned the sketch she was working on toward him, taking in the rough draft of a globe with connecting W's, the initials the travel agency had requested. "And so talented, too. It would be a shame to see all this creativity go to waste."

His mocking tone chafed her nerves, but she didn't let it show. "Since you weren't expecting the project on your desk until Friday, is there some other reason you stopped by?"

He stared at her for a long moment, obviously not caring for the way she was trying to dismiss him. "According to my secretary, you haven't RSVP'd for the Christmas party, which is this Saturday. Certainly you weren't going to miss the biggest bash of the year?"

She resented the sanctimonious way he chastised her. She hadn't planned on attending the party, mainly because she didn't relish the thought of having any outside-of-the-office contact with Louden, but he was making it difficult to refuse.

"I've been so busy, I forgot to respond." The excuse was handy, and served its purpose. "Consider this my confirmation."

"For one or two?"

Uncomfortable with the direction of their conversation, her mind grappled for another convenient excuse...and came up blank.

His pale gaze slid pointedly to the ring on her finger. "Two," she said quickly. "There'll be two of us attending the Christmas party."

Surprise registered in his eyes, and was quickly replaced by skepticism. "Ah, we finally get to meet the elusive boyfriend."

What had been an innocent white lie to keep Louden at bay was now becoming a tangled mess. He hadn't pressed her, accepting the fact that she had a boyfriend in the beginning, but as the months wore on, she suspected he had his doubts. This was the first time he'd made any direct reference to his suspicions.

"What's his name?" he asked casually.

She stared at Louden, her mind freezing. "Uh, excuse me?" The phrase bought her some time, but not much, she knew. She hadn't thought to create a name for her fictitious boyfriend.

"Your boyfriend," he repeated slowly. "He does have a name, doesn't he?"

"Well, yes, of course he does." *A name, Teddy. Pick a name!* At the moment she couldn't even think of one of her three older brother's names!

"Then what is it?" he persisted. "My secretary needs it for the place settings. We can't have just *anybody* finagling their way into the party."

Teddy's chest hurt and her head swam. When she finally realized that she was holding her breath, she let it out in a rush. "Well, maybe I should check with...him. We'd talked about the Christmas party, but quite honestly, he didn't actually say yes, so we probably should discuss it further." She offered Louden a placating smile.

Louden's eyes narrowed slightly, and a smile curled the corner of his mouth.

Very casually, he picked up her hand, the one with the diamond and ruby band, and ran his finger over the embedded jewels. She tried not to visibly shudder at his touch.

"You know, Theodora," he said, deliberately using her full name as a way of maintaining his superiority. "For a woman who claims she's committed, you sure do have a hard time remembering the simplest things about your beau. Maybe he's not as important as you'd like everyone to believe."

She yanked her hand from his grasp. "That's ridiculous."

A pale eyebrow lifted, expressing those doubts.

Desperation coiled within her, and she seized the only name in her mind. "Austin," she blurted.

He looked taken aback by her outburst, and somewhat confused. "Pardon?"

She summoned as much confidence as she could and injected it into her voice. "My boyfriend, his name is Austin." The threads of her white lie were taking on a decidedly black cast. Hell, since she'd incriminated Austin this much, she decided to go all the way and worry about the consequences later. "Austin McBride."

Sliding off the edge of her desk, Louden straightened and glanced down with enough arrogance to make her uneasy. "Well, I suggest you give him a call and find out for certain if he'll be attending the Christmas party with you. My secretary needs a firm head count by the end of today."

Teddy watched Louden leave the office, and knew she'd backed herself into a corner. What she needed was her own personal fantasy man, a fake boyfriend who would establish territorial rights so Louden Avery would back off and see her as a professional, someone well qualified for that promotion. Austin McBride, fantasy for hire, was the man to help her accomplish that goal.

Drawing a deep breath, and hoping Austin could be persuaded to be her date for an evening, she reached for the phone and dialed the number she'd memorized from his business card. The line connected and rang, then a recorder clicked on.

"You've reached Fantasy for Hire," Austin's voice came over the line, just as deep and rich as she remembered. The sexy, masculine tones spread warmly through her, touching places that had been untouched for too long. "Leave a message and I'll get back to you as soon as possible." A long beep followed.

"Hi, Austin," she said, just as Louden walked back into her office, a file folder in his hand. Their gazes met from across the room, the interest in his eyes enough to tell her he'd heard her greeting. She had no choice but to finish her message to Austin.

She hadn't counted on having an audience, and had only planned to leave a brief, impersonal message for Austin to return her call. Louden's unexpected presence changed all that, forcing her to make up a believable monologue as she spoke.

"It's, uh, Teddy," she continued, while her mind latched on to an idea. "I'm calling about the Christmas party this Saturday. Have you decided to go? Since you're not home, I guess we'll talk about it tonight. We're still on for drinks, right? I'll see you at seven at the Frisco Bay." She dropped her voice to a husky pitch, lowered her lashes coyly for Louden's benefit and added, "And later on tonight I'll wear that adorable Stetson you gave me for my birthday, as long as you promise to wear your chaps."

She hoped that last intimate reference would serve a dual purpose—to give Louden the impression that she and Austin were, indeed, intimately involved, and to leave no doubt in Austin's mind who, exactly, the caller was. Austin didn't seem the type to forget a woman's name, but she wasn't taking any chances. The Stetson would identify her, if her name failed to spark his memory.

Whether or not he showed up to meet her was a whole other issue.

Her face burning at her brazenness, she hung up the phone, hoping Louden would mistake the heat scoring her cheeks as a lover's glow.

Setting the file in her in-box on the corner of her desk, he stared at her for a long moment, making her uncomfortable. Even after hearing her one-sided conversation, he still didn't believe her. She could see the doubt in his expression, could detect his skepticism in the set of his rigid posture.

Wanting to deflect his suspicion, she pasted on a smile. "He wasn't home, but go ahead and tell Janet to add two more to the guest list."

"Are you sure about that?" he asked, too quietly for her peace of mind.

She suspected his question went much deeper than her

certainty about the party. "I'm sure. Go ahead and put Austin's name down as my date. He'll be there. I can be very...determined when it comes to something I want." She shot one of his double-edged comments right back at him.

"Sometimes, determination isn't enough," he retorted meaningfully.

"He'll be there." She wished she felt as confident as she sounded. Truth was, she feared Austin would hear the message on his answering machine and write her off as a nutcase.

"Very well, then. I look forward to meeting the elusive Austin McBride."

She folded her hands on top of her desk and met his gaze levelly. "He's looking forward to meeting you, too."

"WHERE HAVE YOU BEEN? You were supposed to be home an hour ago."

With a large, flat box tucked under one arm and his other wrapped securely around a green plastic container holding a small, wilting Douglas fir tree, Austin maneuvered his way through the front door of the old Victorian home he and his older brother, Jordan, had inherited when their parents died fourteen years ago. For the past eight years he'd occupied the house by himself, ever since Jordan had moved to Los Angeles to pursue his architectural career. Eight years of coming and going as he pleased, without worrying about accounting for his whereabouts.

Some habits, especially Jordan's protective instincts toward his little brother, died hard. Jordan had always been the dependable, levelheaded one of them, but then he'd had the responsibility of raising a sixteen-year-old hellion thrust upon him when he, himself, should have been tasting freedom at the tender young age of eighteen. A huge obligation like that tended to make a man out of a child fairly quickly, and Jordan had taken the role of guardianship very seriously. Too seriously, Austin thought, refraining from the urge to remind his brother that he was a big boy and had proven that he could take care of himself.

Pushing the door closed with his shoulder Austin shoved the potted fir into his brother's hands, giving him no choice but to take the plant.

"Well?" Jordan persisted, following Austin into the adjoining living room where he put the Douglas fir on the corner of the brick hearth. "Where have you been?"

"You haven't even been home a week and already you're starting to sound like a wife, big brother." Setting the package on the settee that had once belonged to his great-grandmother, Austin cast an amused glance Jordan's way. "A wife is the last thing I need in my hectic life."

Jordan shoved his fingers through his thick, dark brown hair and grimaced. "Sorry," he said, releasing a deep, frustrated sigh. "It's been a long, boring day. And you did say you'd be home at four, and it's after five."

Austin's gaze touched on the fifty-year-old grandfather clock in the corner of the room and noted the time. "Hmm, so it is."

Despite his brother's annoying habit of keeping tabs on him, Austin experienced a bit of sympathy for Jordan. After giving an L.A. architectural firm eight years of loyalty, and being promised a partnership in the firm, he'd been bypassed when they'd promoted a relative instead. Jordan had been used and lied to, and if there was anything he abhorred, it was dishonesty. Two weeks ago he'd quit the firm, packed up his belongings and moved back to San Francisco to reevaluate his life.

In Austin's estimation, Jordan had too much idle time on his hands. And until his brother decided which direction he wanted to take with his career, Austin pretty much resigned himself, and his life, to his brother's scrutiny.

Jordan was still waiting for an answer. Austin liked making him suffer—goading his brother had always been a favorite pastime, one he'd missed over the past eight years. Shrugging out of his sports jacket, he draped it over the back of the settee. Then he went to work loosening his restricting tie.

"I'm late because I had an afternoon appointment with a client that ran longer than I'd expected," he told Jordan as he pulled the tie from around his neck and added it to the jacket. "But I got myself a signed contract for a landscaping project I bid on a few weeks ago for a new restaurant. The job came in at a little less than fifty grand."

"That's great." Jordan's hazel eyes brightened with pride and genuine excitement for Austin's success. "Congratulations."

"Thanks." Austin was still feeling the elation of having outbid the other landscaping companies. This one project, coupled with half a dozen other smaller projects he'd been awarded recently, would keep a steady paycheck coming in. "And after that, I picked up the Christmas present I was supposed to get last night."

Jordan flicked his finger at the big, fat red bow topping the package wrapped in bright holly paper. "Ah, and who might this be for?"

Austin watched Jordan pick up the box, and knew from experience what was coming next. "It's for you, and don't shake it—"

The order came too late. For all Jordan's seriousness, he had an insatiable curiosity, which included trying to guess what his gifts were. The contents of the box rattled as he gave it a brisk jostling, and his eyes lit up like a little kid's.

Austin's stomach pitched as he imagined the delicate, expensive pieces belonging to the specially ordered model of the Bay Bridge breaking into minuscule segments. "Dammit, Jordan," he growled as he grabbed the box and rescued the collector's edition from Jordan's abuse. "I'm serious. It's very fragile."

A grin quirked Jordan's mouth. "What did you do, get me a set of wineglasses?"

"Very funny." Austin put the gift next to the potted fir.

Jordan came up beside him and cast a hand at the withering tree. "And please don't tell me you're going to try and pass this off as a Christmas tree. It's pathetic, Austin."

"That's why I chose it." Austin smiled and shrugged. "It needed a home, and we couldn't celebrate our first Christmas together in years without a tree."

"So you picked the scrawniest one you could find?"

"I didn't think we'd need anything big and elaborate, considering it's just the two of us."

Jordan shook his head at the sad state of the tree. "I hope it holds up for the next week."

"A drink of water, a string of garland, and it'll be fine." Austin turned toward Jordan and cuffed him on the shoulder. "And for what it's worth, I'm glad you're home for the holidays."

Jordan returned the sentiment with a smile. "Yeah, me, too."

"So, any important calls today?" Austin asked as they headed into the kitchen. Opening the refrigerator, he snagged a can of root beer for himself and popped the top.

"That depends on how you define 'important.'" Jordan's tone turned rueful. "I overheard a message on your Fantasy for Hire line that was certainly interesting."

Austin was used to customers leaving odd messages and requests on that line. When you were in the business of fulfilling fantasies, you got some doozies. Though Jordan was aware of the basic operation of the business, his mind was still boggled by the appeal of Fantasy for Hire, and the outrageous requests he'd been privy to the past week.

Jordan smirked. "You must have made quite an impression last night at your cowboy gig."

The can of soda stopped midway to Austin's lips, and he lifted an eyebrow at his brother. "What makes you say that?"

Jordan's grin broadened. "The very personal message someone left on the Fantasy for Hire line for you."

Interest piqued, Austin set his soda on the counter and headed into an adjoining room that had once been a dining room. Now, it was a no-frills, makeshift office for Fantasy for Hire, consisting of an old, scarred mahogany desk and a battered metal file cabinet. The surface of the desk was cluttered with order forms, and a large appointment book opened to the month of December. Judging by all the fantasies filling it, it certainly *was* the month for giving.

The phone, with an answering machine and fax attached, sat on one corner of the desk. A digital display indicated he had eight messages waiting for him. He sighed. So much for relaxing after a long day at McBride Landscaping—it looked as if he'd be spending the next hour or so returning calls and scheduling his guys.

He rewound the tape, wondering who'd left the message Jordan seemed so amused with. The only thing he could think of was that the women who'd hired him for Teddy's cowboy fantasy had been disappointed with his act. According to the description he'd given them when they'd placed the order, they'd been expecting a blond-haired, blue-eyed cowboy. If they'd been dissatisfied with him or his performance, he'd refund their money.

"Oh, by the way," Jordan added as he stepped into the office behind Austin. "You've got a seven o'clock appointment tonight."

Austin jerked his gaze to Jordan, certain his brother was joking. Seeing that he wore his serious, older-brother expression, Austin's hopes for a peaceful evening dwindled even more. "I told you last night I wouldn't be performing anymore, not unless I absolutely have to."

"You performed last night," Jordan pointed out.

"That was due to circumstances beyond my control. I had no choice."

"You don't have much choice for tonight, either." Jordan displayed no sympathy for Austin's plight. "You were specifically requested."

Frustration coiled through Austin, and he dragged a hand along his jaw. "I thought you said you didn't want to have anything to do with the business, including taking calls during the day."

"I don't, and I didn't." A humorous sparkle entered Jordan's eyes as he pushed his hands into the front pockets of his pleated trousers. "I heard the message while the caller was leaving it. Seems that filly you played cowboy for last night took a hankering to you. She requested a repeat performance for tonight."

"Teddy?" The name, which had invaded his thoughts all day, slipped from Austin's lips almost involuntarily.

"Teddy..." Jordan repeated the word as if testing it, then nodded. "Yeah, I believe that's what she said her name was."

Easing himself into the chair behind the desk, Austin frowned. Despite the chemistry that had charged between them, Teddy didn't seem the type to brazenly pursue a man, especially when a ring on her finger indicated she was committed to another. Then again, he could have pegged her all wrong. It wouldn't be the first time he'd been led astray.

Punching the play button on the recorder, he listened to four requests for fantasies before her voice finally drifted out the phone's speaker.

"Hi, Austin," she said, then hesitated a few moments before continuing. "I'm calling about the Christmas party this Saturday. Have you decided to go? Since you're not home, I guess we'll talk about it tonight. We're still on for drinks, right? I'll see you at seven at the Frisco Bay."

Though her voice was strong, he grasped another thinly veiled emotion in her tone. *Desperation.*

She continued in a sexy, husky voice, "And later on tonight I'll wear that adorable Stetson you gave me for my birthday, as long as you promise to wear your chaps."

The recorder beeped at the end of her message, and Austin hit the stop button before the next caller could speak. He sat there, feeling both confused and fascinated by what he'd heard.

Jordan chuckled. "If that isn't a line to inspire fantasies, I don't know what is."

Austin silently agreed with his brother's comment, considering the provocative images that had leaped into his mind, of Teddy wearing nothing more than the Stetson he'd given her, and a head-to-toe flush tinging her skin. Oh, yeah, he was certainly inspired. And intrigued. More than he'd been in years.

But beyond the sexy innuendo of Teddy's final remark, there was more to her words than a flirtatious come-on. Though she'd spoken in an enticing tone of voice, he didn't get the impression that she was asking for a personal fantasy. On the contrary, he got the feeling that her entire message was a setup of some sort, and that last line had been her way of prompting him to remember who she was.

As if he could forget.

When he'd arrived home last night, he'd been keyed up from the performance and that rare, inexplicable connection he'd experienced with Teddy Spencer. And though he'd tried, he hadn't been able to shake his mental image of her soft smile and those incredibly sensual brown eyes that had shown him glimpses of shyness, and the potential to be a little reckless. She was off limits, for so many reasons, but his mind had a hard time accepting that fact. Despite his best efforts to maintain his professionalism, she'd taken a hot shower with him, then continued to distract him while he'd attempted to concentrate on an estimate he was preparing for an upcoming landscaping bid. She'd so totally consumed his thoughts that he had no choice but to abandon the figures and call it a night. And that's when he'd done the unthinkable—he'd taken her to bed with him and succumbed to the most erotic dreams he'd had since puberty.

And damn if he didn't wake up hard and aching, and wanting her.

Suddenly, the familiar stirring started again, deep in Austin's belly. He drew a deep breath, gradually released it and firmly focused on the present situation. He knew nothing about a Christmas party, or a date for drinks tonight. She'd left no phone number, no way of contacting her to find out what her strange message was all about.

Remembering the silent plea he'd detected in her voice, he found he couldn't bring himself to stand her up.

"So, what's this about a Christmas party this Saturday?" Jordan asked, his expression curious. "Do you think maybe she needs a guy to play Santa Claus?"

Austin curbed the impulse to let out a hearty *ho, ho, ho.* As amusing as he found Jordan's suggestion, gut instinct told him Teddy's request had little to do with needing a Santa for hire.

"I haven't the slightest idea what she's talking about," he admitted, then allowed a slow, devilish smile to form. "But I do intend to find out."

3

HE WAS LATE. Either that, or Austin McBride had no intention of meeting the woman who'd left such a brazen message on his answering machine. Despite how much Teddy was depending on Austin to help her out of her predicament, a part of her wouldn't blame him if he didn't show.

Feeling anxious, Teddy glanced at her wristwatch for the fourth time in the past ten minutes and made the decision that she'd give Austin until 7:30 p.m. before she resigned her post in the Frisco Bay.

While she waited, she sipped her sparkling water and looked over the patrons in the lounge, most of whom she knew as regular customers of the bar. Thanks to Brenda's and Laura's outgoing personalities, Teddy was now acquainted with many of the men on a first-name basis. She'd even politely turned down a date or two from a few of the single males present tonight. Luckily, the men who frequented the Frisco Bay were out looking for a good time, no strings attached, and didn't seem to take rejections personally.

As the minutes ticked by, Teddy found herself perusing the guys in the bar tonight, sizing each one up as a potential date for Saturday's party should Austin not show. None sparked her interest. Certainly none compared to Austin McBride's gorgeous looks and charisma. His confident appeal was precisely what she needed to convince Louden that he could never measure up.

"Hey, Teddy," a female acquaintance sitting at a nearby table called. "Isn't that your cowboy?"

Every female head in the establishment turned toward the entrance of the Frisco Bay to get a glimpse of last night's attraction. Teddy included.

Relief at seeing him mingled with a heady dose of awareness that prickled along the surface of her skin. "Yeah, that's him."

There was no trace of the cowboy who'd come calling the previous evening, but then Austin didn't need a western costume to accentuate that athletic body of his. A dark brown knit shirt showed off his broad shoulders and molded to a muscular chest and flat belly. The khaki pants he wore weren't nearly as tight as the jeans he'd donned last night, but they looked just as good, in a more polished, urban sort of way.

What the women in the place recognized, Teddy suspected, was Austin's head-turning features, that tousled thick brown hair that made a woman want to run her fingers through the warm strands, and those striking green eyes that flirted and seduced with a simple sweep of those long, dark lashes.

"Is he back for a repeat performance?" another woman asked hopefully.

"Not a public one," Teddy replied, startled by the spurt of jealousy she felt. She certainly had no claim to Austin McBride, but that thought didn't diminish the fact that she didn't want to share him with the dozen other women in the bar who were anxious to see him shed his clothes.

Eyebrows rose curiously, and Teddy reached for her drink, refusing to elaborate on her comment, though it was true. Austin's performance would be a private affair, one he'd be keeping his clothes on for.

He found her sitting at the bar and headed in her direction, carrying himself with a relaxed self-assurance that was at once appealing and unwavering in confidence. Oh, yes, Teddy thought breathlessly. Austin was exactly what she needed to convince Louden that he was overstepping boundaries. Austin came across as the type who wouldn't tolerate another man infringing on his territory.

Her stomach fluttered as his gaze locked on hers, making her feel as though she was the only woman in the place—certainly the only woman he was interested in, despite the hungry looks and moist-lipped smiles being cast his way by the other women in the bar. The intensity with which he focused on her was a good indication that he could convince anyone that he was her devoted lover.

By the time he reached her, Teddy knew she wouldn't be able to find a better man for the job than Austin McBride. He was *the one.*

"Hi," she said, gracing him with a smile she hoped didn't look too enthusiastic.

She'd saved the padded stool next to her for him, and he slid into the vacant seat, his own smile adorably contrite. "I'm sorry I'm late. I had a scheduling conflict I had to resolve that took longer than I'd anticipated."

"Lots of fantasies to fulfill, hmm?" she teased.

For a moment he appeared harried, then covered up that fleeting glimpse with something resembling reluctant resignation. "More than I can handle."

Considering Austin epitomized a woman's fantasy, she wasn't at all surprised that his services were in demand. "Well, I'm just glad you showed up," she said gratefully. "After that message I left on your answering machine, I was certain you'd think I was a nutcase."

"Not at all." He braced his forearm on the bar, humor dancing in his eyes. "I was intrigued by your message, to say the least. So was my brother."

Her heart flipped at the thought of another McBride brother as gorgeous and charming as this one. Before she could ask Austin if his brother was in the business, too, Jack, the bartender, sidled up to their seats from across the mahogany surface of the bar, recognition glimmering in his eyes. Drying a beer glass, he grinned broadly at Austin.

"So, what will it be, cowboy?" Jack asked in a feigned western drawl. "The regular?"

"That would be great." Austin tossed a five-dollar bill toward Jack with a comment to keep the change before Teddy could offer to pay for his drink. "Make it on the rocks this time."

"You got it, just so long as you keep your clothes on tonight." Jack set a glass with ice in it on the pouring pad in front of him, then used a spigot to fill the glass with a dark, fizzing liquid. "It took me hours to settle the women down after you left last night. Since you've walked in, the crowd has gotten a little restless."

Austin's gaze slid to Teddy, irresistibly warm and sexy. "My business here tonight is all pleasure."

She shivered at the deep, rich timbre of his voice, and that flirtatious smile that tempted and teased. He seemed totally unaware of the interest he was generating, unaware of all the eyes and ears tuned into them. Teddy, on the other hand, grew increasingly uncomfortable with everyone's scrutiny. What she needed to ask Austin wasn't something she wanted up for public speculation.

"Would you mind if we took that table in the corner so we can have a little privacy?" she asked.

If he was surprised by her request, he didn't show it. "Not at all."

Grabbing her purse and drink, she led the way, nearly jumping out of her skin when he settled his hand lightly at the base of her spine. It was a common gesture, yet with Austin his touch had a decidedly possessive air to it. Not to mention enough heat to penetrate her tightly knit sweater and make her feel branded.

Once they were seated next to each other, he glanced at her and smiled. "So, what can I do for you, Teddy Spencer?"

The answers that filled her mind were shameless, and she gave herself a firm mental shake that knocked those naughty thoughts out of commission. "I have a problem, and I'm hoping you can help me out."

"In what way?"

Currently, her problem seemed to be her inability to think straight while those sexier-than-sin eyes were trained on her. "I need a fantasy..." Startled that such a reckless request could tumble from her lips, she grappled for another line. "I mean, I need a fiancé..." She groaned at her blunder, felt the rising warmth in her cheeks, and didn't trust herself to speak further.

His grin turned a bit more wicked, giving her the distinct impression he was enjoying her slip of the tongue. "The fantasy I could help you out with, since I have plenty of experience in that area, but I'm afraid being your fiancé is out of the question. I hardly know you."

The humorous note to his voice made her relax. She leaned back in her chair, wiped her damp palms on her black denim jeans and decided to try again. For all her business savvy with clients, she was beginning to sound like a bungling idiot with the one man who could help her pave the way to a smooth future with Sharper Image.

"Let me try this again," she said, drawing a deep, calming breath. "I need someone to pose as my steady boyfriend and escort me to a party."

He stared at her, the enjoyment of the previous moment

fading from his expression. "I don't run an escort service."

The disapproving edge to his voice was enough to alert her she'd crossed a professional line with him. "Of course you don't," she amended hastily. "I never meant to imply that you did, but isn't it at all possible that I could hire you for a few hours? You do hire out by the hour, don't you?" The words, once they were out, sounded like an indecent proposal.

He shook his head, his dark hair gleaming from the low lights in the lounge. "I'm really sorry," he said, his voice filled with genuine regret, "but I can't help you out. I make it a rule never to mix fantasy with reality."

She found his comment odd, but didn't have the time to worry about what, exactly, he meant. She bit her bottom lip, realizing she had no choice but to put her pride on the line.

Taking a swallow of her sparkling water to ease the dryness in her mouth, she met Austin's gaze. "I'm embarrassed to have to admit this, but I told my boss that my boyfriend's name is Austin McBride."

Austin's dark eyebrows rose in surprise, and a grin quirked the corner of his mouth. "Really?" he drawled.

She held up a hand, certain he was writing her off as a basket case. "I know what you're thinking—"

"You have no idea," he murmured, his low, amused voice stroking along her nerves. Seeing the mischievous glint in his eyes, she decided maybe she *didn't* want to know what he was thinking.

Hopelessness settled over her. Could this meeting get any worse? she wondered, dragging her hand through her loose hair to pull it away from her face. She'd failed in her attempt to proposition Austin for an evening, and even her humiliating admission about blurting out his name to Louden hadn't swayed him.

As much as she hated to admit it, she needed Austin McBride. Her career at Sharper Image depended on him. Only he could knock Louden down a peg or two. And having Louden witness the sexual chemistry between them would be a bonus, too. One night, five hours max. A few tender touches and intimate glances, and once the Christmas party ended they'd go their separate ways.

It was the perfect arrangement.

But first, she had to convince Austin. "Maybe I should explain my situation from the beginning, so my request for your services makes sense."

"Please do." After taking a drink of the dark liquid in his glass, he reclined back in his chair, clasped his hands over his flat stomach, and regarded her with rapt curiosity.

She glanced around the lounge to make sure they didn't have an audience, and was relieved to find the excitement caused by Austin's appearance had subsided. Returning her attention to the man next to her, she forced her thoughts on business. "I started with Sharper Image, the company I'm currently working for, a little less than a year ago. I was hired as a layout assistant, and within six months was promoted to a graphic designer position with my own accounts."

"Do you like your job?"

Austin's unexpected question threw her concentration off stride and the genuine interest he expressed warmed her. Nobody ever asked her about her job, whether she enjoyed it or hated it. When she'd enrolled in college, her brothers and parents hadn't taken her goals seriously, and wrote off her dream of becoming a graphic designer as a hobby. They'd hoped her engagement to Bartholomew

Winston would settle her down, but that brief period in her life had only served to make her realize how important her independence was to her, and how badly she wanted to make it on her own.

The disappointment of their daughter embracing a career over marriage was still a sore spot with her parents. Talking about her job and how much she relished the mental stimulation and challenges wasn't something the older Spencers encouraged when she visited, and so Teddy had learned in order to keep peace, she kept quiet.

"I love my job," she told Austin, taking advantage of his interest. "Especially the creative freedom I have as a graphic designer. I design letterheads, logos, brochures and develop advertising strategies for businesses and corporations. I've got a flawless record with Sharper Image, and my reviews have been glowing. Recently, the position of senior graphic designer became available. Considering my experience, degree and performance the past year, I'm a prime candidate for the promotion."

She paused for a moment, making sure she still had Austin's attention. "This is where it gets tricky. Louden Avery, who is my boss and creative director over my department, sees me as a candidate of an entirely different sort. Ever since I started at Sharper Image, he's made a few comments that leave me feeling uncomfortable. A few months after I was hired, I told him I had a steady boyfriend, thinking he'd lose interest. He backed off for a while, but it hasn't lasted."

Austin's gaze flickered to her left hand, which rested on the armrest nearest him. "So, you don't really have a boyfriend then?" he asked, looking back up at her.

She recalled the odd comment he'd made last night, about having to explain the Stetson to her boyfriend, and realized the ring on her finger had given him the wrong impression. "No, no boyfriend. The ring is merely a diversion, but it's losing its credibility. When Louden pressured me about bringing my elusive boyfriend to the Christmas party and demanded a name, yours was the first one I came up with."

He smiled. "I'm flattered."

Hope bloomed within her. "Flattered enough to stand in as my date Saturday night?"

Indecision touched his expression, and before he could succumb to his reservations, she reached out and grasped his hand, stopping just short of dropping to a begging position in front of him. She was desperate, yes, but she didn't want everyone in the Frisco Bay to witness her despair. "One night, Austin, please? I'll pay you enough to make it worth your while."

A young woman at a nearby table turned and looked at them, shock and curiosity brightening her eyes. Belatedly, Teddy realized how incriminating her words had sounded.

Teddy glared until the woman turned back to her own companion. So much for being discreet! Before the night was over, word would probably spread through the Frisco Bay that Teddy Spencer had propositioned her cowboy. She hadn't said what that one night entailed, but knew the other woman was thinking along the lines of sex. When Teddy returned her gaze to Austin, silent laughter glistened in his eyes.

"Please," she begged in a low whisper.

"Let me get this straight," he said, leaning forward so he could brace his forearms on his knees. In the process, he switched the position of their hands, so hers was enveloped in the warmth of his. "If I decided to do this, you'd expect me to act like your steady boyfriend?"

She nodded eagerly and dampened her bottom lip with her tongue. "Yes."

His fingers drew lazy, sensual patterns on her palm, sending scintillating tremors up her arm. That frisson of awareness settled in the tips of her breasts, tightening her nipples into hard, sensitive peaks. "And give everyone the impression that we're intimately involved?"

The sensations he was evoking were as intimate as anything she'd ever experienced. He stroked softly between thumb and index finger, a skillful caress that made her pulse race. "Ahhh, yes," she managed to say, though she sounded as if she was out of breath. "The, um, more people that think we're intimately involved, the better."

The corner of his mouth kicked up in a seductively wicked smile that matched his deep, rich voice. "You want Louden Avery to have no doubt in his mind that we're a couple well and truly committed."

"Exactly." Unable to stand his provocative caresses any longer she gently withdrew her hand from his. "One night should do it, as long as you think you can be convincing."

"Oh, I don't think that'll be a problem." On him, confidence was an incredibly sexy thing. "I specialize in fantasies. I have a feeling this performance will come naturally."

Judging by the thrum of desire that had just shimmered between them, she suspected he was right. She flashed him a cheeky grin. "Well, I don't expect you'll have to take off your clothes for this performance."

He smiled. "You don't know how relieved I am to hear that."

"So you'll do it?" she asked anxiously, needing to hear him say yes.

Instead of the positive response she anticipated, he

grew serious, studying her intently. "Why is this so important to you?"

Teddy resisted the urge to throttle him. The man certainly wasn't an easy sell, though she had to admit it was nice to know he wasn't in it just for the money. It was as though he cared, and it had been a long time since someone had cared enough to listen to her.

"I want that promotion, and I want it awarded to me on my own merit. I've worked hard and I deserve that position without having to compromise my morals. Since Louden is making the process so difficult, proving to him that I'm in an intimate relationship will put an end to his pursuing me."

He tilted his head, his gaze kind, but concerned. "And you think if Louden believes you're unavailable, that will make him judge the candidates for the position fairly?"

The doubt in his voice was unmistakable, but she refused to dwell on it. "That's what I'm hoping. I'm the most qualified for the position, but I refuse to submit to Louden's tactics to get it."

She saw him wavering despite his concern, and panicked. She couldn't lose him now! Giving in to that damned vulnerable emotion named desperation, she dug into her purse, withdrew her leather checkbook case and wrote a check for his services in the amount of one thousand dollars before he could refuse her.

Tearing off the signed voucher, she pushed it across the small cocktail table toward him and lifted her chin in sheer determination. "If that isn't enough for your time, I'm willing to pay more."

Austin glanced at the check, noted the staggering amount she'd offered, and realized how deeply her tenacity ran. She wasn't making him a reckless, frivolous offer—she was proving she'd take whatever risks necessary to secure her future.

He wasn't comfortable accepting that much money, even though it appeared Teddy Spencer could easily afford it. She didn't even bat an eye at the amount she'd written on the check. Although she came across as very down to earth in attitude, her well-bred sophistication couldn't be hidden beneath a pair of black jeans and a Christmas red sweater that outlined perfect breasts. The cut of her hair was a shoulder-length classic, the kind of style that fell softly around her face and made the best of her naturally elegant features. Flawless half-carat diamonds winked in each earlobe, an exquisite, but understated touch. And she had the moves of wealth, too, walking and gesturing with a grace that was refined and private-school polished.

On a distant level, those particular signs made him uneasy, but he didn't know enough about Teddy to make any assumptions. He only had tonight's encounter to judge her by, which had given him a mixture of fascinating contradictions to sort through.

Confidence radiated from her, yet he'd detected touches of vulnerability, too, as if she had to struggle to maintain that hard-won self-assurance. That quality he understood and identified with—he'd grappled with similar emotional challenges after his parents died. He'd only been sixteen, and it had taken him years, along with Jordan's guidance, for him to finally understand the security he'd lost. His landscaping company gave him the financial stability he sought, but he was still searching for that emotional connection that offered the deep solidity he craved.

"Is it enough?" she asked, her voice quiet, but firm with purpose.

Picking up the check, he studied it, deciding the name Teddy suited her much more than her stuffy given name, Theodora.

He shifted his gaze back to her and smiled. "Actually, this amount is a bit high, considering I don't have to take my clothes off."

The fingers she'd knotted in her lap relaxed and the tense set of her shoulders eased. "Then consider it an easy night. And I'll pick up any other expenses you might incur." She stuffed her checkbook back into her purse and began issuing instructions, as if fearing any lapse in conversation might give him a chance to come to his senses and refuse her proposition. "The Christmas party is a black-tie affair, so you'll be expected to wear a tuxedo. I can set up an appointment for you to see my tailor, who also rents tuxedos—"

"Actually, I already have a tuxedo," he said, interrupting her. She blinked at him in surprise, and he grinned. "It's quite a common fantasy."

"Oh, of course." Her face now becoming a shade of pink, she ducked her head and rummaged through her purse to retrieve a pen and notepad. "Cocktails are at six-thirty, so you can pick me up at six. Here's my address, home phone number and my number at the office if you should need it."

He listened to her ramble on, waving a hand in the air while giving him verbal directions to her condominium complex. He watched her mouth as she talked, enjoyed the way she used her tongue to sweep across her lush bottom lip and wondered what it would be like to kiss her. The urge to find out what she tasted like was strong, and his body tightened in response.

She placed a hand on his arm, her light touch severing his erotic daydreams. "I can't thank you enough for agreeing to this." She looked out of breath, which is what he suspected ended her rambling—the need for oxygen.

Diamonds and rubies sparkled on the hand resting on his arm. That ring might have dissuaded her boss's advances, but in the process, the band also gave every other man she met the impression she was unavailable. He found Teddy's motive for wearing the ring very interesting, and wondered if it served a dual purpose for her.

He met her gaze and gave in to curiosity. "Tell me something, Teddy. You're a beautiful, classy woman. You must have been able to find a date for Saturday, someone you might know who could have convinced Louden that you're off the market. So why me, a total stranger?"

She hesitated. Deep reservation passed over her features, along with a flash of defiance, adding yet another dimension to her already intriguing personality. "I don't want anything complicated," she told him. "And since we really don't know one another, our transaction can be strictly business. One evening, then we go our separate ways."

She made it sound so easy, but he was beginning to think the situation wasn't so cut-and-dried. Certainly pretending to be Teddy's lover had enormous appeal, but his interest went beyond a single night of flirtatious overtures and provocative glances.

He found Teddy attractive, sexy, vivacious and full of secrets he wanted to discover. Despite the fact that he had little time for a relationship in his busy life, he wanted Teddy Spencer. He wanted to see if the heat between them was as electrical as it felt, wanted to kiss her and feel her come alive in his arms as she had in his dreams last night...

"Well, it's getting late," she said abruptly, and reached

for her purse. "And I need to get up early in the morning."

"So do I." He stood, and while he waited for her to follow suit, he folded her check and put it into the front pocket of his pants. He still wasn't sure what to do with the money, but he'd already decided that Saturday night was going to be his treat. It would be his pleasure to be Teddy's lover. "I'll walk you to your car."

They left the bar together with the stares of the patrons following them out the etched-glass door. Outside, the air was December chilled, and the parking lot was barely illuminated by two streetlights. He followed her to a sedate white Honda Accord, parked in a shadowed area of the lot.

Standing by the driver's side, she turned to face him. "I guess I'll see you Saturday night." She thrust out her hand. "Thanks again."

She was so polite, and so determined to keep their agreement on a business level. He had other ideas. Slipping his hand into hers, he tugged her closer. The unexpected movement caused her to waver off balance. She put her hand out to catch herself, and her palm landed on his chest. She gasped, a sexy little intake of breath that warmed his blood and told him her attempt at formality had just slipped a serious notch.

Her luminous brown eyes were wide and searching. "Austin?"

Her voice trembled, not with protest, but with the thrum of desire. Slipping his fingers around her wrist, he stroked his thumb over the wild pulse beating at the base of her palm. Her skin was soft and warm, and when he took a deep breath, he inhaled a subtle, floral fragrance that awakened something hot and primitive within him: *The need to make her his.*

"You know," he murmured, his tone vibrating with low, husky nuances. "Since we'll be pretending to be lovers, there's something we should get out of the way before Saturday."

"What's that?" she asked, her voice a whisper of anticipation.

"Our first kiss." He lowered his head, and experienced a heady rush of excitement when she automatically tipped hers up to meet him halfway. Inches away from claiming her mouth, he hesitated, drawing out the moment to marvel at her acquiescence. He hadn't even touched his lips to hers, but they were parted and ready. Her breathing was eager and expectant, turning him on and making him think of the needy, purring sounds she'd make if he ever had the pleasure of making love to her.

She didn't play coy, didn't shy away from the blatant sexual energy between them. She didn't try to suppress something as basic and natural as desire and he liked that about her. The awareness had been building all evening, in subtle ways, and both of them were ready for the culmination of all that smoldering tension.

Closing the breath of space separating them, he dropped his mouth over hers, and didn't even have to cajole his way past her incredibly soft lips. His tongue glided deeply, sought and found hers, and tangled playfully. The kiss was slow and silky, soulful and honeysweet. He took his time exploring, tasting and seducing, until leisurely sweeps of his tongue were no longer enough to satisfy the deep, vital hunger gripping him.

He needed...*more.*

She gave a soft, frustrated moan that echoed his own growing impatience, and the hand on his chest curled into a tight fist. Heat coiled low in his belly and spread outward, ruthlessly reminding him just how long he'd gone without the softness of a woman's body to ease his more baser needs.

He didn't want any woman but Teddy. Teddy with her soft, sexy sighs and incredibly generous mouth...

In a flash he was hard and hungry and feeling more than a little wild. And reckless enough to take their encounter one level higher.

Keeping his mouth slanted across hers, he maneuvered her a step back so she was crushed between her car and his body. A gasp caught in her throat, then rolled into a seductive moan when he released her wrist and gripped her hips in his hands, pulling her intimately closer, if that was at all possible considering their bodies were fitted as tightly as a man and woman could get...from breast, to belly, to thighs.

Blood pounded in his ears and rushed along his nerve endings. Her hands slid up his chest and around his neck, then her fingers delved into his thick hair, urging him to give more. His mouth opened wider over hers, and that's when the tenure of the kiss changed, turning demanding, erotic, and so wet and hot he knew if they didn't stop he was going to spontaneously combust.

He broke the kiss, and she whimpered in protest.

"Damn," he muttered, trying to regain his composure. He hadn't meant for things to get so out of control, never expected her to be so soft and giving. Taking a deep, calming breath that did nothing to ease the racing of his heart, or diminish how much he wanted her, he glanced down at Teddy.

She looked stunned, a little disoriented and completely aroused.

Tenderly, he ran his knuckles down her soft cheek and traced the line of her jaw with a finger, slowly drawing her out of her sensual trance. "At least no one at the

Christmas party will doubt the chemistry between us."
He couldn't help the masculine satisfaction in his voice, or
the pleased grin curving his lips.

She visibly swallowed and gave him a shaky smile.
"That's exactly what I'm counting on."

4

"I CAN'T BELIEVE you let him kiss you." Teddy frowned sternly at her reflection in the bathroom mirror as she chastised herself for surrendering to Austin's kiss three days ago outside of the Frisco Bay. The fact that she'd thoroughly enjoyed Austin's advances and openly participated in that sensual embrace was another issue she'd lectured herself on, all to no avail.

"Well it wasn't *me* who instigated that kiss," she argued with her twin image as she dusted blush lightly across her cheekbones.

A mocking smile curved her evil twin's mouth. "You certainly didn't do anything to stop him, now, did you? In fact, I distinctly remember you kissing him back with shameless abandon. You didn't even try to resist him."

"Fine!" Teddy's cheeks heated, making the blush she'd just applied unnecessary. Tossing her cosmetics into the bathroom drawer, she lifted her chin, meeting her own gaze defiantly. "I wanted that kiss, okay?" She'd wanted much more than just his lips on hers, but she wasn't about to admit *that* out loud.

Drawing a deep, steady breath, she swept her hair into an elegant chignon, allowing a few wispy curls to escape around her neck and face. "Tonight, you're going to behave yourself, Teddy."

She rolled her eyes at herself. "Of course I'm going to behave myself! This is a business deal, nothing more."

She pushed rhinestone-studded pins into the mass of hair at the nape of her neck to hold it in place. With a decisive nod of her head, she ended the absurd discussion and headed into the adjoining bedroom.

Her reflection followed, appearing in her dresser mirror, taunting her.

Glaring, she slipped out of her robe, leaving her scantily clad in black lace panties. Ignoring her image, she retrieved a pair of smoke-hued, thigh-high stockings from her lingerie drawer, lifted a slender leg onto the edge of the bed and rolled the hose up her calf to her thigh. She snuck a peek at her alter ego in the mirror and experienced a prick of annoyance at the perception glimmering in her eyes.

"What?" Teddy demanded haughtily, securing the other stocking.

"Business deal, hmm?" her reflection murmured. "What about Austin posing as your lover? He's going to touch you, pretend intimacy..."

Teddy's breasts swelled and tightened at the thought of enduring Austin's amorous advances. Gritting her teeth in frustration, she grabbed her black slip dress from where she'd laid it on the bed, carefully shimmied it over her head and wriggled the clingy fabric over her hips. She adjusted the rhinestone straps holding up the snug bodice and crisscrossed along her bare back.

Reaching for her diamond stud earrings, she slipped them into her lobes, then backed up to get a full-length view of how she looked for the Christmas party. Elegant, yet sophisticated and confident. Precisely the self-assured look she wanted to achieve.

She gave herself an approving nod. "Just keep your mind on that promotion, Teddy, and off your gorgeous date, and you'll be fine."

"Good luck," her twin smirked. "Considering you melt when the guy just looks at you, you're gonna need it."

She jammed her hands on her hips and scowled. Before she could issue an argument, a knock sounded at the door, and her stomach rolled...with nerves, anticipation and a bubbling excitement that didn't bode well for her peace of mind. Squelching the flurry of butterflies taking flight in her belly, she hurried out of the bedroom to the condo's front door. One glance through the peephole at the gorgeous man standing in the hallway and her heart rate skyrocketed while her knees turned to mush.

Willing a calm composure, she opened the door, momentarily dizzied by the enticing spice cologne drifting her way. Her gaze took in his tailored tuxedo, deriving immense pleasure from the way the suit complimented a body she knew to be virile and incredibly honed. The dark color accentuated his chiseled good looks and gave him a mysterious air. She dabbed her tongue along her dry lips, fantasies aplenty leaping to mind. It wasn't hard to imagine him stripping off that jacket for some woman, releasing the black bow tie, ripping off his shirt...

An amused smile curved his mouth, reaching his warm, moss-green eyes. "Hi," he murmured, pulling her from her inappropriate thoughts.

"Hi," she replied, unable to help the husky quality of her voice. The man simply made her feel breathless, reckless and too aware of herself as a woman. The sensation unnerved her, because she couldn't afford that kind of distraction.

She cleared her throat. "You look..." Scrumptious, sexy, to-die-for. All apt descriptions, but she settled for, "great."

Flirtatious eyes appraised her just as thoroughly as she'd assessed him, lingering appreciatively where the black dress dipped to reveal a swell of cleavage, then downward to the hem that ended just above her knee. The journey upward was just as lazy, and just as arousing to her senses. "So do you."

Promotion, promotion, promotion. The chant ran through her mind like a litany.

"Come on in," she said politely, stepping back to let him enter. She closed the door, then followed him into the adjoining living room. "I just need a few more minutes, and then I'll be ready to go. Make yourself comfortable."

Just as she would have turned to escape to her bedroom for a last-minute lecture, he reached into the front pocket of his trousers and withdrew a piece of paper. "Before we leave, I wanted to give this to you."

She eyed the yellow slip he held toward her. "What's that?"

"A receipt for my services."

"Oh." Tentatively, she took the proof of payment, not sure she wanted a reminder of her desperation.

"And I hope you don't mind," Austin continued, "but I donated the thousand dollars to the Children's Hospital in your name."

Startled at his announcement, she lifted her gaze to his face, noting his earnest expression. "Why?"

His broad shoulders lifted in a casual shrug. "Because I thought the money would be better spent on people who need it. And besides, it is the season of giving."

"Yes, it is," she agreed, overwhelmed by his generosity, and his sincerity, when most of the men she knew would have pocketed the money without a second thought. She folded the receipt and tucked it into her purse on the countertop separating the living room from the small kitchen. "Thank you. That was incredibly thoughtful and selfless."

His easy, charming smile dismissed her compliment. "Tonight is on me. Merry Christmas, Teddy."

Touched by his gesture, she closed the distance between them, wanting to express her own gratitude with a chaste, affectionate kiss on the cheek. At the last moment, he turned his head slightly, and her lips brushed his in a soft, infinitely gentle kiss. Her eyes momentarily closed at that tender touch, a rush of warmth suffused her veins and her lips parted on a sigh.

Austin didn't take advantage of her unconscious offering. His mouth hovered above hers, his breath warm and scented with mint as it caressed her lips. Desire twisted through Teddy, sharpening her senses. He didn't touch her, didn't initiate a deeper kiss, like the one she yearned for, yet her body sizzled with awareness.

Heart pounding, she slowly lifted her lashes. Her gaze collided with the unmistakable heat in his eyes—a hunger that told her she was playing with fire, and if she was bold enough to close the inches separating their lips, he'd be happy to oblige her, and more.

She considered the temptation, anticipated the pleasure and weighed the consequences of involving herself with this man who was proving to be more of a distraction than she'd counted on. Deciding she couldn't allow her attraction to Austin to interfere with her goals, she abruptly stepped back, severing the moment. But the magnetic pull was still there, shimmering in his eyes, tugging her toward the promise of sexual satisfaction, and something deeper and more intimately connected.

The ache within her intensified.

"I'll, uh, be ready in a few minutes," she said quickly, then retreated down the hall. Enclosing herself in her bathroom, she pressed her back against the door, took deep breaths to still her racing pulse and didn't dare look in the mirror for fear of encountering her evil twin again.

"Promotion, promotion, promotion," she chanted like a prayer.

AUSTIN STROLLED around Teddy's modestly decorated living room while he waited for her to return, unable to wipe the smile from his face. There was something incredibly sexy about Teddy when she was flustered. Add to her appeal her generous, straightforward personality and that little black dress she was wearing, and he was finding himself hard-pressed to resist her.

Judging by that near miss they'd just had, it appeared she was struggling to suppress the same craving for him. And if a little kiss made her nervous, he wondered how she was going to handle the evening, with him making sure everyone at tonight's party went home with the impression that he and Teddy were intimate. Surely she realized that illusion meant more than stealing a kiss or two?

He looked forward to those stolen kisses, those subtle caresses. And he was hoping by the end of the night she'd realize that there was something very personal and real between them.

That was the main reason he'd donated the money she'd paid him. Not only was he uncomfortable taking such a huge chunk of change for something he wanted to do, but also, he absolutely refused to be a paid escort. Donating the check to a good cause seemed the perfect solution, for him to keep his conscience intact, and to take away Teddy's excuse that she couldn't mix business with pleasure.

Tonight, he was her date, accompanying her to the Christmas party of his own free will. Pleasure was the fundamental purpose of this evening, and he planned to make sure Teddy experienced her fair share.

The phone on the countertop rang, breaking into Austin's thoughts. He glanced down the short hallway toward her bedroom, wondering if Teddy was available to pick up the line.

The phone pealed again, loud and insistent.

"Teddy?" he called, and got no response. Figuring she was in the bathroom, he decided to do her a favor and take the call, just in case it was important.

He lifted the cordless receiver to his ear on the third ring. "Hello?"

Silence greeted him.

He frowned. "Hello?" he said again, more assertive this time.

"Hi, uh, is Teddy there?" a female voice tentatively asked.

A girlfriend, Austin guessed, and could only image what the other woman was thinking. "Yes, she is, but she's busy at the moment. Can I take a message?"

"Who is this?" the voice queried.

Austin hesitated. He had no idea how many people thought Teddy was seriously involved, especially considering she wore a ring all the time. So he decided to stick with the story he and Teddy had come up with.

"This is Austin McBride, her boyfriend."

"Her boyfriend?" The woman sounded genuinely delighted. "I didn't realize Teddy was seeing someone. Isn't it just like her to keep something like this a secret from the family?"

Her family? Austin cringed. "Could I ask who is calling?"

"This is Teddy's sister-in-law, Susan," the woman said,

introducing herself in a bubbly tone. "Have you and Teddy been seeing each other for long?"

Austin glanced down the hallway, hoping to see Teddy coming to his rescue. No such luck. "We've been friends for a while," he hedged. *Three days, at least,* he mentally justified. "And just recently started dating." How recent, he wasn't going to elaborate on.

"Wow!" Susan released a gust of light laughter. "The rest of the family is going to be thrilled. Teddy hasn't dated since her breakup with Bartholomew." She paused as if realizing she'd revealed too much. "Uh, she did tell you about Bart, didn't she?"

Austin could feel himself being ensnared in a trap of his own making, and wasn't sure how to escape. "Oh, absolutely," he replied, certain he was sinking in way over his head.

"Her parents still haven't gotten over the fact that she'd throw away a great catch like Bart to pursue a career. But for as long as I've known Teddy, which is going on ten years now, she's always been the rebellious one in the family. Not that I blame her, considering how stifling her parents and brothers have been," Susan added wryly.

All Austin could manage was a quick nod, because Susan-the-talker didn't give him a chance to respond to her steady monologue.

"Don't get me wrong," she continued. "I love my husband and the rest of the Spencer clan, but they are a bit old-fashioned in their thinking. It took me years to knock some sense into Teddy's brother and make him realize that I'm an independent woman, who doesn't need to be coddled. Teddy has been trying to prove the same thing to her family, but they just don't seem to understand how important it is to Teddy to make it on her own, without the influence of Spencer money or connections."

Austin's stomach bottomed out, and old bitter memories threatened to swamp him. So, Teddy did come from money, as he'd suspected. He couldn't help but wonder how someone blue collar like him might fit into her group of Ivy League friends and family. Not well, as he'd learned from experience.

"So, in some ways, I'm not all that surprised that Teddy has been keeping you all to herself. When I was dating Teddy's brother, Brent, I was the one subjected to the Spencers' scrutiny. It wasn't fun."

Austin pinched the bridge of his nose with his thumb and forefinger. As fascinating as he found Susan's rundown on Teddy's family, he didn't like hearing this stuff secondhand. Or maybe he just didn't care for what he was hearing, period.

"Well, Susan," he managed to break into the conversation when the woman finally took a breather. "Is there some kind of message I can pass on to Teddy for you?"

"Oh, of course!" She laughed brightly. "Here I am, talking your ear off, and I'm sure Teddy is waiting on you. Tell her that Christmas Eve dinner next week is at six, and to be on time. I think she shows up late just to annoy her mother." Humor, and understanding, followed up that statement.

Austin grinned at Teddy's display of defiance, and jotted down the message on a notepad situated near the phone. "Will do."

"You will come with her, won't you?" Susan asked hopefully.

Austin's insides clenched tighter. "I don't think I'll be able to make it," he lied. Not only was he certain he wouldn't fit in with the Spencer clan, he didn't think Teddy would appreciate him tagging along to meet Mom and Dad. "I have other plans."

"Surely you can make the time to meet Teddy's family, even if it's just to stop by for a few minutes?"

Was it his imagination, or was there an underlying disapproval in Susan's words, like what kind of guy was he if he couldn't even make the effort to meet his girlfriend's family? He felt like a schmuck, yet it was his own fault for allowing the fabrication to stretch so far. But how was he to know who knew Teddy's secrets?

The excuse did nothing to ease the twinge of guilt he experienced. "I'll see what I can do," he compromised. Hopefully, Teddy would be able to smooth out the mess he'd made of things.

"Great." Enthusiasm infused Susan's voice. "It was nice talking to you, Austin. I'm looking forward to meeting you."

"Uh, same here." He disconnected the line before anything more could be said. Hanging his head, he shook it in dismay.

Hell, what had he done?

"I heard the phone ring while I was in the bathroom." Teddy's voice drifted from down the hall as she approached the living room. "Did you catch the call, or did the answering machine pick it up?"

"Don't I wish," he muttered.

"Excuse me?"

Straightening, he faced her, just in time to see her drop a lipstick tube into her small black beaded purse and snap it shut. During her absence she'd put on a pair of heels, lengthening those eye-turning, shapely legs of hers. She looked like a million bucks.

The irony of that assessment wasn't lost on him. "That was your sister-in-law, Susan."

Teddy came to an abrupt halt in front of him. "Oh?"

He thrust his hands into the front pockets of his trousers. "And she's now under the assumption that I'm your boyfriend."

"Oh, no," she groaned.

"I'm sorry, Teddy," he rushed to apologize, not that his own regret could make up for any damage he'd done. "I had no idea who you told about your 'significant other,' and it came out before I found out who she was."

He expected her to be angry, or at the very least upset, but she appeared more worried than anything. "Oh, it's not all your fault. I adore Susan, but even if you hadn't said you were my boyfriend, she would have come to that assumption on her own. Everyone in my family wants me to find a decent man and settle down." The disgust in her voice was evident.

He didn't get that impression from Susan, but then again the other woman had been quite enthusiastic about Teddy being in a relationship again. Family dynamics were a curious thing.

"I'll just give her a quick call and explain our one-night arrangement." Startled by the sound of her own words, she amended hastily, "I mean, set her straight about our business deal."

So, she was back to *business*, was she?

Teddy reached for the phone, tucked it next to her ear and punched in a series of numbers. With a forced lightness, she added, "The last thing I'd want is for my entire family to think I'm seriously involved with someone. They'd be all over you like piranhas, picking you apart, piece by piece."

Her analogy wasn't a pleasant one, but it served to remind him of where they stood with one another—on opposite sides of the tracks. There was no way her family would approve of a guy who fulfilled women's fantasies, and was struggling to maintain a landscaping business.

A frown creased Teddy's forehead, and with a deep sigh, she set the phone back into the cradle. "The line's busy." She gave her gold watch a quick glance. "I'll have to catch up with Susan later. We need to get going."

Picking up her black shawl from the couch, she settled it over her bare shoulders and headed for the door. Minutes later, they were in Austin's black Mustang, following Teddy's directions toward the Bay area.

Silence filled the interior of the vehicle, except for the low volume of mellow music drifting from the speakers. Austin glanced briefly Teddy's way. She sat in the passenger seat, staring out the window, quiet and subdued. Reserved even. Was she mulling over the conversation he'd had with her sister-in-law? Or was she more worried about the Christmas party ahead?

"So, who is Bartholomew?" he asked, voicing the one question that had been on his mind since Susan mentioned him.

"I'm gonna strangle Susan," Teddy muttered darkly.

A grin quirked the corner of Austin's mouth. "Pardon?"

"Bartholomew Winston is a past mistake," she said succinctly, without looking at him. "And one I'd rather not talk about."

The resentment in her tone was unmistakable. "All right," he conceded, now even more curious about this mystery man of her past, and what had happened between them.

Again, silence reigned. As Austin exited the freeway and neared the hotel where the Christmas party was being held, the more tense Teddy seemed to become. He no longer suspected that her uneasiness stemmed from Susan's call. It was all about the promotion she was up for—if Louden fell for their little game.

Tonight would tell.

Pulling the Mustang under the valet awning, he put the car in park and turned toward Teddy. He touched her knee, his fingers rasping along her silky stockings, and she jumped in response. She jerked her luminous gaze, now filled with anxiety, to his, but the slight tremble he felt where his fingers lay idly against her thigh told him she was very aware of him, and the intimacy of their situation.

He tilted his head, regarding her with genuine concern. "Hey, you okay?"

She moved her leg out of his reach, dislodging his gentle touch. She gave him a smile that appeared more like a grimace. "Sure, I'm fine," she said in a tone too bright and chipper.

He stared at her for a long moment. Beneath all that forced cheerfulness, there was something incredibly vulnerable about her—not that he'd expect an independent career woman like Teddy to ever admit to such an emotion. No, she wanted to be strong and confident, and in control. A part of him understood that. Respected it, even.

"Teddy," he whispered, wishing she'd ease up and relax around him. Otherwise, Louden Avery would know he was a fraud, and that revelation would defeat Teddy's purpose. But before he could express his concerns, a young man opened her door and offered a gloved hand to help her out of the car.

Austin sighed, gave his vehicle over to valet and met up with Teddy on the curb. Settling his palm on her lower back, he ushered her through the automatic glass doors that whooshed open for them. She stiffened, but didn't protest the hand resting so familiarly where her spine ended and the curve of her bottom began. There was nothing inappropriate about the way he touched her, yet he got the distinct impression that she would have preferred he didn't.

Knowing she was forcibly resisting what was between them, irritation gripped him. She was nervous, he acknowledged that, but she was giving off the wrong kind of vibes if she expected everyone to believe they had something going on. He wasn't sure what to do about her remoteness, but his mind mulled over various ideas.

They followed the signs for Sharper Image's party through the lush, expensively decorated lobby to a glass-enclosed elevator that shot straight up to the thirty-second floor and overlooked the bay. Stepping into the lift behind Teddy, Austin pressed the only button available that would take them to the tower's ballroom.

The elevator, dimly lit inside to make it easier to look outside, slowly made its ascent, giving the occupants plenty of time to admire their surroundings. The evening sun had set almost an hour ago, but nightfall allowed them to appreciate the expanse of water beyond, and the twinkle of lights from the boats coasting along the ocean. A quarter of the way up, they had a breathtaking panorama of the Bay area.

The atmosphere was romantic, made more so by the intimate four-by-four cubicle that confined them. Teddy didn't seem to notice, or appreciate, the ambience. She stood at the brass bar lining the thick glass enclosure, her gaze lost on something off in the distance.

"Nice view," Austin commented, in an attempt to strike up a conversation. Standing behind her, the view *was* fantastic—she had a nice bottom that deserved a lingering glance.

"Hmm," was Teddy's noncommittal response.

He rubbed a finger along his jaw and tried again. "It sure is an awfully long ride up. The possibilities of what a couple could do with all this time is endless." He didn't disguise the sexy innuendo in his voice.

"Hmm." His suggestive comment didn't faze her.

Frustration nipped at him. If he couldn't even shock her into acknowledging him, then they were in for a disaster of an evening.

Finally, the right idea came to him, the shock value of which would either set her off, or wind her down. He was hoping for the latter result.

Reaching back to the button panel, he pressed the red one marked Stop. The elevator came to a slow, whirring halt somewhere between the lobby and the thirty-second floor.

She spun around, panic etching her features. "Oh my God! We're stuck!"

A lazy, unrepentant grin kicked up the corner of his mouth. "I deliberately stopped the elevator."

Her jaw dropped. "You what?"

He knew she'd heard him, so he didn't bother wasting precious time by repeating himself. Instead, he closed the distance between them and braced his hands on the brass railing on either side of her hips, trapping her between the cool glass and his solid body.

A small, stunned gasp escaped her lips, and her body immediately grew rigid. "What are you doing?" she demanded.

His grin widened at her haughty tone, but it certainly didn't deter him. Moving closer, he pressed his thighs against hers, and pushed a knee between her legs to keep her in place. "You know, if you don't relax and shake off that tension that has been building since we left your place, we're never going to convince your boss that we're lovers."

Teddy dampened her bottom lip with her tongue, then

released a long breath. "You're right," she admitted, and clearly expected him to release her.

Not totally convinced of her acquiescence, which he suspected was an act for his benefit, he kept her pinned right where he had her. The shock value was about to increase. "What do you think, Teddy, should we start the party off with a bang and give your co-workers something to talk about?"

Even in the dim light illuminating the interior of the elevator, he could see the suspicion in her gaze. "What do you mean?"

He caressed the back of his hand down her soft cheek, strummed his fingers along her neck, watching as her deep brown eyes darkened with the first stirrings of desire. "How about a quickie at eighteen floors up overlooking the bay?"

She gasped in wide-eyed astonishment, then a burst of laughter bubbled up from her chest. "You're outrageous!"

He chuckled along with her. "You have to admit that the thought is thrilling...maybe just a little bit."

She glanced down at their position, and he wondered if she realized what a perfect support that brass bar behind her would be. It would be just a matter of lifting her dress, removing her panties, unzipping his pants and letting her sit on that sturdy bar with her back braced against the window as he slid inside her and she wrapped her legs around her hips...

He nearly groaned at the erotic image, and knew she was thinking the same thing by the way the pulse at the base of her throat fluttered.

She swallowed hard, and managed a slight shake of her head. "Austin..."

He conceded to the warning in her voice, but the erection straining the front of his trousers wasn't nearly so co-operative. "Okay, making love here and now might be a bit too scandalous, but how about necking? That's pretty harmless." Before she could object, he skimmed a hand along her hip to her waist and stroked her belly with his thumb through the silky material of her dress. "I want to kiss you, Teddy," he murmured huskily as his head dipped toward hers. "Will you let me?"

Her chin lifted, bringing her lips closer to his. "We shouldn't."

He smiled. "Maybe we should, to help get rid of all that tension."

She pulled back a fraction and frowned at him. "I'm perfectly fine."

"Yeah, that's why you get skittish every time I touch you," he said wryly. "Just enjoy the evening, Teddy. Have fun with the charade. When I touch you, flow toward me..." Lifting his hand, he smoothed it down her spine in a luxurious caress. She softened, her back arching until her lush breasts brushed his chest. Even through his starched shirt, he could feel her tight nipples, and it nearly drove him crazy. Keeping his thoughts centered and focused on her, he lowered his mouth near the side of her head. He breathed in that floral fragrance that was uniquely hers, and his senses spun. "When I whisper in your ear, close your eyes and think of something sexy, so it looks as though I'm murmuring naughty things to you, even if I'm just asking you to pass the salt."

She let out a long breath, and he pulled back just far enough to look at her face. Her eyes were closed, her expression soft and slumberous, certainly relaxed. Her body followed suit, growing pliable beneath his slow caresses. "Can you do that, Teddy?" he asked.

Her lashes lifted, revealing a need as strong as the one

coursing through his veins. "Yeah," she whispered, her voice sultry-soft in the darkness of the elevator.

"Good." He marveled at his ability to remain so calm when his hormones were clamoring for something more elemental. "And how about that kiss? Can I have it?"

Seemingly seduced by all that had come before, she lifted a hand, sifted her fingers through the hair at the nape of his neck and brought his mouth to hers. "Yes," she murmured, and gave him a deep, hot, tongue-tangling kiss more potent than any aphrodisiac.

Passion rose swiftly to the surface, shattering his control. He gripped her hips and rocked urgently against her, swallowing her gasp when his thigh moved upward and pressed against sensitive flesh.

He had to have her. His palm touched her silken thigh, the same moment a shrill ring filled the small cubicle, vaguely penetrating the fog of desire that had settled over him. By the second ring, Austin realized the emergency phone in the elevator was the annoying culprit.

Reluctantly dragging his mouth from Teddy's, he reached behind him, managing to grasp the receiver without moving away from her. They were both breathing hard from their erotic encounter, and he had to take a deep, steady breath before speaking.

"Yes?"

"This is security," a gruff voice came over the line. "Everything okay up there?"

His gaze locked on Teddy's, noting the combination of amusement and arousal glowing in the depths of her eyes. Feeling incredibly daring, he trailed a finger along the rhinestone strap holding up her dress, down to the dip of cleavage swelling from the bodice. "Just taking a little time to enjoy the fabulous view."

Teddy let out a giggle at his double-edged comment,

and she slapped a hand over her mouth to contain her laughter, her eyes sparkling. He managed, just barely, to contain his own chuckles.

"Keep the elevator moving, buddy," the security guard grumbled, sounding put out. "We've got a crowd of people down in the lobby waiting their turn."

Hanging up the phone, he flipped the Stop switch, and his stomach dipped as the elevator glided upward. "We still have a long way to go," he said, coming back to her with a wicked grin. Framing her face between his palms, he murmured, "Where were we?"

He didn't wait for her to answer, but resumed the kiss that had been interrupted with as much enthusiasm as before. Mouths met, lips parted and tongues entwined silkily. No resistance, just a mutual hunger that spiraled and tightened between them.

He kissed her with deep thoroughness, wanting to brand the moment in her mind forever. And in return, he was equally seduced. She was soft, provocative and sweeter than honey. He wanted to taste her skin to discover other flavors and contrasts, ached to run his tongue across the breasts crushing against his chest. He wanted to be anywhere but in a roomful of people, making polite conversation and pretending to be Teddy's lover.

He wanted to be the real thing.

Too soon, he ended the sensual embrace, but the thrum of desire remained.

"Damn," he whispered as he rested his forehead against hers, his body inflamed and his mind fogged. "Are you sure you don't want to ride the elevator back down and try a quickie?"

She groaned, and when he lifted his head, he saw that she was smiling. And much more languidly than before. Her rich brown eyes shone bright with passion, her cheeks wore a rosy hue, and her lips were swollen from their shared kiss.

Male gratification flowed through him. He'd achieved his goal. Not only did Teddy Spencer appear to be a woman well satisfied, but her tension had abated.

She blinked, and as if finally coming out of some drugging trance, her gaze blossomed with worry. Her fingers fluttered to her hair, which Austin had been careful not to touch. "Oh, God, I probably look a mess!"

Grinning, he adjusted her shawl to cover the shoulder it had slipped from during their interlude. "You look beautiful. A little tousled, but certainly convincing."

"I can't believe we did that!" she admonished gently.

He stroked his hand over her bottom, and felt her shiver. Her uninhibited response pleased him. "And just think, we've got the whole evening ahead of us." He winked at her.

The elevator came to a slow, smooth stop at their final destination, a soft *ping* announcing their arrival. Knowing they only had seconds to compose themselves before they greeted the entire staff of Sharper Image, Austin straightened his tuxedo jacket, then at the very last moment slid his hand possessively into Teddy's.

The insulated doors whooshed open and a dozen curious eyes clamored to sneak a glimpse of the couple who had stopped the elevators midway up to the thirty-second floor. Austin watched eyebrows rise, grins split across surprised faces and murmurs of disbelief and amusement filter from one person to another.

Austin's mouth curved into a roguish grin, purposely adding fuel to the rampant gossip that would no doubt circulate during the Christmas party and establish him as the man in Teddy's life.

5

TEDDY HELD her head high and stepped from the elevator with Austin, intensely aware of everyone's inquisitive stares, and the disheveled way she looked after her interlude with Austin. With Austin gently squeezing her hand and offering silent support, she felt surprisingly confident, and reckless in a purely feminine sort of way. As nervous as she'd been about tonight, Austin had erased a good portion of her anxiety with humor, charm, and hoards of sex appeal—the latter of which had her female colleagues giving the good looking man at her side a thorough, effusive once-over.

Back off, girls, he's taken.

Tonight, Austin was *her* fantasy for hire, and she planned to enjoy the evening, as he'd suggested. The more comfortable she was around Austin, the more convincing they'd be as a couple.

After introducing him to the group of single females obviously waiting to meet him—and watching as he dazzled everybody with his sexy smiles and irresistible personality—they decided to mingle. Over one hundred and fifty employees were present, from mail-room clerks to the top brass, all decked out in their holiday finery. She searched for Louden, but in the crush of people she didn't see him.

The mood was festive, with a hired band playing upbeat Christmas tunes during the cocktail hour. Being that this was Teddy's first company Christmas party, she was highly impressed with the show Sharper Image put on.

The ballroom was elaborately decorated for the Christmas season, with garland, holly and mistletoe aplenty. Eight-foot noble firs, gaily decorated in sparkling lights and pretty ornaments, scented the room with traditional pine. Centerpieces of bright red poinsettias and tapered cream candles adorned each table, and lacy snowflakes sprayed with a shimmering incandescent powder hung from the ceiling, giving her the illusion of being in a winter wonderland. The effect was enchanting.

Teddy made sure she introduced Austin to as many people as she could, from the CEO of the company to the front-end receptionist, and watched in amazement as he effortlessly established a male camaraderie with the men, and beguiled the women, while making it apparent, with an affectionate glance, an intimate comment, that he was completely devoted to her. During the moments when they were alone, he'd touch her possessively, run his fingers over her bare back and down her spine, keeping her body in a constant state of awareness. More daring, he'd lean close and murmur bawdy comments and jokes in her ear that caused her to blush, laugh out loud, and made them look as though they shared intimate secrets.

Teddy found herself so wrapped up in his attention, even she had to struggle to keep from blurring the lines between reality and fantasy.

"Would you like something to drink, sweetheart?" Austin asked. He'd spent the past five minutes charming two women Teddy worked with, and as much as she didn't want to be alone with the duo answering a barrage of questions, she *was* getting thirsty.

She gave him a warm, private smile for her co-workers' benefit. "I'd love a wine spritzer."

His large, hot palm casually slid over her hip to her waist, pulling her close to brush his lips across her cheek. A tremor of response rippled through her, and her breath quickened.

Striking green eyes glittered with devious pleasure when they met hers again, testimony that the rogue was relishing every minute of their performance. "I'll be right back, so don't go far."

As if her weak knees would allow her to wander off!

Barb, Sharper Image's payroll clerk, sighed wistfully, not bothering to conceal her lust as she watched Austin walk away. "What an absolute doll he is, Teddy."

"Mmm," Karen, an accounts rep, agreed, shaking her head in wonder and envy. "Where have you been hiding him all this time?"

"I, well, uh..." Teddy grasped a ready excuse while absently twisting the diamond and ruby band on her finger. "Austin's work keeps him incredibly busy. It's a wonder *I* get any quality time with him."

Barb scoffed at that. "Come on, Teddy, the guy is crazy for you. From what I've seen tonight, not to mention the rumor circulating about a little incident in the elevator, he doesn't come across as a man whose been too neglectful."

Fire burned Teddy's cheeks.

"I have to agree," Karen said, her eyes sparkling merrily over the rim of her champagne glass as she took a sip.

Knowing there was no sense denying what both Barb and Karen wanted to believe—what she, herself, needed them to believe—she didn't bother to correct their assumption. "Would you two stop, already?"

"We're just jealous," Barb admitted good-naturedly. "He's personable, totally into you, and has a body to die for. And he's probably rich to boot."

Teddy didn't think Austin wallowed in wealth, but she

imagined his "Fantasy" services kept his bank account amply filled. "Oh, he does quite well for himself."

"What does he do, anyway?" Karen asked curiously.

Panic raced through her, pumping up the beat of her heart until she could hear it drumming in her ears. Good Lord, they hadn't discussed a respectable occupation! "He's a...broker." Well, he definitely qualified as such, she reasoned, considering he solicited his services, and those of his other employees.

"Oh," Barb said, looking suitably impressed. "Like an investment broker?"

"Uh, yes," Teddy said, going with the suggestion because nothing else sounded better. Feeling herself flounder in unfamiliar territory, she searched frantically for Austin, and found him over at the service bar talking to the vice president of the company while he waited for their drinks.

In an attempt to divert the conversation before she complicated the situation further, she turned back to Karen. "So, I hear you're planning a surprise baby shower for Catherine Johnson in Marketing after the new year. What can I do to help?"

A few moments later, Austin finally returned. He handed her the wine spritzer, then took a sip of his own drink, which looked suspiciously like root beer. Grateful for the interruption, she told Karen and Barb that she'd get the rest of the details on the baby shower next week at work, and quickly maneuvered Austin in the opposite direction before his cover was blown. Finding a secluded, unoccupied arbor decorated in colorful twinkling lights and Christmas greenery, she finally stopped and faced him.

He waggled his dark eyebrows at her. "Eager to find a

dark corner to have your way with me, eh?" His voice was low and tinged with all kinds of wicked innuendo.

Her stomach dipped, but she resolutely ignored the sensation. "No, I—"

He abruptly cut off her words with a kiss that happened so spontaneously she didn't have a breath of a chance to stop those tantalizing lips from covering her own. Gaining her equilibrium, she jerked back, nearly spilling her wine spritzer down the front of her dress.

"Austin!" she admonished, not exactly shocked at his audacity, considering how bold he'd proven to be. But still, they'd given the employees at Sharper Image plenty to gossip about without giving them a public display, too!

"What?" He blinked at her, a picture of little-boy innocence. "You're standing under the mistletoe, and anyone watching would expect any self-respecting boyfriend to take advantage of the situation."

Skeptical, she glanced up at the arbor they stood under. Sure enough, a sprig of mistletoe dangled above her head.

Without permission, he came back for a second sampling, this time curling his long fingers around the nape of her neck and using his thumb to tip her chin up and keep her mouth firmly locked beneath his. He parted her lips with one silken stroke of his tongue, and she tasted heat, and the sweet flavor of root beer.

Losing all sense of time and place, she gave herself over to his soft, compelling kiss. The man stole her sanity, made her want things she'd convinced herself she didn't need in her life and threatened her hard-won independence. He made her feel too reckless, and entirely too needy.

Desperate to pull the situation back into perspective, she placed a hand on his chest, feeling the strong, steady beat of his heart beneath her palm. To anyone watching, the gesture looked like an affectionate caress, but he immediately picked up on her cue. Or maybe it was her panic he sensed.

With a low growl that reverberated deep in his chest, Austin lifted his head, his eyes glowing with unsuppressed hunger. "I suggest we finish this later, when we don't have an audience."

Certain that intimate comment was meant for their viewers' ears, she nodded, the only intelligible gesture she could manage at the moment.

"They have got to be the most romantic, in-love couple I've ever seen," Teddy heard some woman say from behind Austin.

They'd certainly fooled everyone, she thought with a grimace. Hopefully, Louden would be just as convinced.

Arm in arm, they strolled away from the arbor. "You're an investment broker," she whispered in a low voice to Austin, and nodded sociably at an older couple who were smiling at them.

"I am?" Amusement threaded Austin's voice.

"As of ten minutes ago, you are."

"How about I own my landscaping business instead?"

She shook her head at him, dismissing his offbeat suggestion. "No, I was thinking more along the lines of something upscale and respectable."

"Respectable?" he echoed, his voice losing that humorous edge of moments before.

Her face flushed. She hadn't meant to insult him. "Well, yes," she hedged. "Saying you're an investment broker is more respectable than announcing you're a fantasy for hire. You weren't around, we hadn't discussed an occupation, and it's the first thing I thought of."

He shrugged, and accepted her choice of career. "Okay. After all, this is *your* fantasy."

She frowned at him, and his choice of words. "No, my fantasy was a cowboy. This is strictly business."

Annoyance flitted across his handsome face, and just when she suspected he was going to issue an argument of some sort, the man she'd been dreading all evening finally approached them. The tension Austin had worked so hard to obliterate quickly spread through Teddy's body, tightening muscles and tingling nerves.

Dressed in the prerequisite black tie, Louden exuded confidence and professionalism, which Teddy supposed appealed to the higher-ups in the company. Louden couldn't have climbed the corporate ladder as high as he had without competence and some personable qualities. What the directors didn't realize, though, was just how poorly he handled employee relations.

Pale blue eyes scrutinized Austin lazily, but Teddy wasn't fooled by his complacent behavior. Even if he was suspicious, he certainly wasn't going to let it show in front of her, or anyone else.

"Hello, Louden," Teddy greeted, trying to maintain a semblance of courtesy.

"Theodora." Louden inclined his head at her and smiled pleasantly. "You look quite lovely tonight."

Ignoring his compliment, she pulled her shawl tighter around her shoulders. "Louden, I'd like you to meet my boyfriend, Austin McBride."

Louden turned his attention back to the man at her side, and Austin extended his hand toward her boss. Their hands clasped in a firm handshake, and Teddy caught an undercurrent of silent rivalry. Austin was clearly staking a claim, and Louden was sizing up the competition.

"Nice to meet you," Austin said, his tone cordial.

Louden didn't return the sentiment. "So, we finally get to meet the man in Theodora's life. Can't say I've heard a whole lot about you. Other than that ring on her finger, Teddy's been keeping you a secret."

"Well, she certainly hasn't kept you a secret," Austin replied meaningfully.

Something dark sparked in Louden's gaze, but he didn't respond. "You must be very proud of her. Theodora has proved herself to be quite a valuable asset to Sharper Image in the nine months that she's been working for the company."

"The woman constantly amazes me with her talent and dedication." Austin slipped his arm around her waist and pulled her close in an open display of support and tenderness. "I'm hoping to see her promoted to that senior graphic design position, where she can really exercise that creative mind of hers."

Teddy discreetly nudged Austin in the side. The man was pouring the praise on a bit thick.

"I'd really like to see her promoted, too, but I have the difficult task of weighing both candidates' proficiency for the position and convincing my superiors of their competence." He sighed, as if the selection process was a burdensome one. "Needless to say, it's been a tough decision."

"I'm sure you'll select the most qualified person for the job." Austin's words were cool, but very calculated.

Louden's expression was just as shrewd. "Without a doubt."

The band announced that dinner was about to be served, and for everyone to find their seats before the buffet began.

"If you'll excuse me, I see a few people I'd like to say hello to before I sit down," Louden said. "You two enjoy the evening, and I'll see you in the office Monday, Theodora."

Once they parted ways with Louden and headed toward their designated table, Austin asked, "Is there a reason why he calls you Theodora when everyone else calls you Teddy?"

"To annoy me, and to make sure I keep in mind his position of authority." The only other person who used her formal name on a regular basis was her prim-and-proper mother, and her brothers when they wanted to antagonize her. "Speaking of which, I'd appreciate it if you didn't directly challenge Louden like that."

Austin clasped Teddy's elbow to escort her through the throng of people. "Yeah, well, someone needs to knock that guy down a peg or two. He's too cocky for his own good, and I don't like the way he looks at you."

She bristled, feeling her defenses rising. For too many years she'd endured coddling and protecting from three older brothers who'd treated her as a weak, vulnerable female. She'd despised every minute of it. That Austin felt compelled to shelter her as well provoked a bit of rebellion, especially when she'd struggled for so long to break free from her family's stifling habits.

"Being my bodyguard isn't your job, Austin," she said emphatically. "All I need you to do is back up the ring on my finger. I'm more than capable of fighting my own battles in the boardroom."

His mouth thinned ruthlessly. "Are you?"

"Yeah, I am." She resented the insinuation that she couldn't look after the situation herself. "I want this promotion on my own merit. My work record proves I'm qualified for the job, more so than my opponent."

Austin didn't look convinced. "Do you honestly believe that introducing your boyfriend is going to stop this slimeball from making future moves on you? Guys like Louden don't stop at minor obstacles like boyfriends. He wants to be in control, and he won't stop until he gets what he wants, which seems to be you. The only way he'll leave you alone is if you press charges."

Teddy's stomach churned as she sat in the chair Austin pulled out for her at their table, but she refused to dwell on his accurate assessment of Louden. "Don't worry, he'll leave me alone," she said, wishing she felt more confident than she sounded.

Austin let the subject drop as they joined the others at the table. Teddy made introductions to the people who hadn't yet met Austin, and valiantly tried to shake off the black mood Louden had cast over them and the evening.

Minutes later, they stood in line at the buffet table, plate in hand. Dinner was a selection of salads, rich side dishes, fancy breads, chicken in a mushroom-and-wine sauce, and prime rib. A quarter of the way down the buffet, Teddy glanced up to find Janet, a buxom redhead who worked in her department as Louden's secretary, staring purposefully at Austin from the opposite side of the smorgasbord. Janet was extremely loyal to Louden, and that alone made Teddy mistrust the woman.

Austin must have sensed the intensity of the other woman's gaze, because he looked up, too—which was all the invitation Janet needed to launch into conversation.

"You look so familiar," she said, tilting her head so her thick mane of curly auburn hair tumbled over her shoulder and lay enticingly just above the breasts straining the too-tight bodice of her spandex dress. "Have we met before?"

The question was harmless, yet an awful premonition made Teddy's stomach dip.

"I don't believe so," Austin replied with a smile, and pressed his hand to Teddy's spine to keep her moving along the buffet line.

Janet managed to stay aligned to them, eyeing Austin with too much interest as she put a croissant on her plate. "I keep imagining you in a police uniform. Are you a cop?"

The spoonful of scalloped potatoes Teddy scooped up missed her plate and would have landed on her shoes if it hadn't been for Austin smoothly intercepting the entrée with his own plate.

"No, I'm a broker," Austin said to Janet without missing a beat. Taking the spoon from Teddy's unsteady fingers, he ladled a small portion of the potatoes onto her dish and murmured, "Be careful, honey, or we're going to have a mess on our hands."

The meaning behind Austin's words wasn't lost on Teddy. She struggled to keep a cool composure when all she could envision was the possible scandal should Austin be exposed. Her reputation at Sharper Image would be tarnished, and no doubt she'd kiss that promotion she'd coveted goodbye.

Austin's answer didn't seem to appease Janet. Ruthless determination gleamed in her eyes. "I was so certain you were a cop."

"You must have him mixed up with someone else you've met," Teddy interjected quickly, desperate to end the interrogation.

"Maybe, but I've got a memory for faces." Janet's gaze flickered dismissively from Teddy, to Austin, scrutinizing him one last time as she waited for the chef to place a slice of prime rib on her plate. "It's going to drive me nuts until I place where I've seen you." The slight curve to her mouth suggested she found Austin a mystery she intended to solve.

Teddy let out a tight breath as they finished their trek through the buffet and headed back to their table. "Tell me she wasn't a Fantasy for Hire customer," Teddy said, knowing her wish was a futile one.

"Unfortunately, I do remember her, though she's not the one I fulfilled the fantasy for," Austin replied wryly. "It was at a bachelorette party a few months ago, and the bride-to-be was marrying a cop, thus my costume. That redhead was more enthusiastic about my performance than the bride."

Teddy groaned at her bad luck. "Hopefully, Janet won't figure out the connection."

"I think as long as I keep my clothes on, we might stand a chance," he said, winking at her.

A burst of dry laughter escaped her throat, but his playful remark didn't completely reassure her.

Clothes or no, Austin McBride had a body and face that most women wouldn't soon forget.

THE CHRISTMAS PARTY was winding down, and Austin loathed for the evening to end, especially since he had Teddy right where he wanted her—in his embrace, dancing close to a slow Christmas ballad that comprised the band's last set.

Despite the fantasy of playing Teddy's lover, he'd enjoyed being with her and wondered if he'd see her again after tonight—no pretenses, just as a man and a woman strongly attracted to each other. The thought appealed to him immensely.

It went against his work ethics to pursue a client, but he'd thrown that restriction out the window the moment he'd agreed to accompany Teddy to her party. The stakes had somehow turned personal for him, his interest in Teddy Spencer stretching beyond business, yet he had no idea where he stood with her.

Before they parted ways, he intended to find out.

He glanced down at the woman in his arms, and found Teddy frowning, her troubled gaze trained on something beyond the parquet dance floor. Following her line of vision, he discovered her watching the redhead they'd encountered at the buffet table a few hours ago, who stood near the service bar conversing with Louden. She'd yet to approach them again, and Austin fervently hoped, for Teddy's sake, that the other woman's curiosity, and tenacity, fizzled. As for Louden, he'd kept his distance as well, but there were times throughout the evening when Austin had caught the man eyeing Teddy in a way that made Austin feel territorial.

"What's on your mind, Teddy?" he asked, surprising himself with just how much he wanted to know about this woman who seemed such a paradox.

She pulled her gaze from the pair, and smiled up at him, a lazy curving of her mouth that attested to her relaxed state. "A cop, hmm?" she murmured, revealing exactly where her mind had ventured. "What's your specialty at Fantasy for Hire?"

"I don't really have one," he admitted, rubbing his thumb over the hand he held against his chest. "Women's fantasies vary, and are very personal. I've been a lifeguard, a UPS deliveryman, a biker. It all depends on the woman, and what turns her on."

The hand resting on his shoulder moved upward, until her fingers touched the hair curling over the collar of his shirt. Her body flowed against his as they swayed to Bing Crosby's "White Christmas." "I bet you look just as good in leather pants as you do in chaps."

"Ah, your fantasy," he murmured. Pressing his palm low on her back, he slid a thigh gently between hers, making their position more intimate, more arousing. "How did I do in terms of fulfilling it?"

She gave him a sultry, upswept look that had him thinking inappropriate thoughts, considering they were still in a public place, surrounded by a dozen other dancing couples.

"You certainly lassoed my attention," she admitted in a sexy, cowgirl drawl.

He felt ridiculously pleased with her confession. "So, what is it about a cowboy that turns you on?"

She gave his question some thought as they danced, her expression soft, her dark eyes luminous. "They're rugged, but chivalrous, which makes them appealing." She shrugged, her gaze meeting his daringly. "And there's just something about chaps on a man that I find incredibly sexy, not to mention the sound of spurs on a wooden floor."

A slow, spiraling heat spread toward his groin. "I'd wear spurs for you, cowgirl," he whispered huskily, honestly.

Her breathing deepened, and through his tuxedo shirt he could feel her breasts swell, and her nipples tighten against his chest, tormenting him.

She touched her tongue to her bottom lip, and as if deciding their conversation was becoming too hot and provocative, she turned the subject back to him. "So, what compelled you to fulfill women's fantasies?"

If she expected an exciting, sensational answer, she was going to be sorely disappointed. "Outstanding loans that needed to be paid."

She nodded in understanding. "And do you enjoy the business?"

"I had more fun when I was younger," he said, thinking back to the inception of Fantasy for Hire, and how a simple vision to earn extra money had exceeded his wildest expectations. Back then, he'd been enthusiastic, enjoying the excitement of each gig. "Now that I've hit thirty, I find I prefer conducting business with my clothes on."

She grinned, and he thought about mentioning his flourishing landscaping business, which had become his main focus, but Teddy's next question didn't allow him time.

"How does your family feel about your profession?" she asked curiously.

"My mother and father are both gone. They died when I was sixteen."

She appeared startled, and immediately regretful. "I'm sorry to hear that. Losing your parents at such a young age must have been extremely difficult."

"Yeah, it was." His mother and father had been good people, very much in love, and totally devoted to their two sons. Their death had shaken up his young world, and if it hadn't been for Jordan's guidance, he very easily would have become a juvenile delinquent. "My brother, Jordan, and I still miss them."

The band announced the final song of the evening, and Bing's tune segued into another ballad without a lapse. Some of the couples dispersed, but Teddy didn't show any signs of wanting to go, so he continued to hold her close as the music played.

Her gaze shone with genuine interest, solely focused on him. "So it's just the two of you then?"

"Yeah. All we have is each other." Austin found he liked talking to her, liked even more that she'd let down her guard to indulge in personal conversation—the getting-to-know-you kind of exchange that real lovers shared. "Jordan is older than me by two years. He raised me after our parents died."

She tilted her head, looking soft, and beautiful, and

very much at ease. "And how does big brother feel about you taking your clothes off for women?"

Austin chuckled, the sound swirling warm and intimate between them. "It's definitely not his cup of tea. Jordan is an architect, and has always been a conservative sort of guy, but he's always been very supportive of me and the choices I've made."

"That's great." Her voice held a wistful quality that reached her eyes. "I wish *my* brothers were that way. Heck, I'd kill for a little support and encouragement from my parents, too."

Austin thought briefly about what her sister-in-law, Susan, had divulged, but still couldn't believe Teddy had ventured into her career alone, without having someone to share each step of success with. "Your family isn't at all supportive of what you're doing?"

She shook her head a little sadly. "Nope. I'm the youngest girl with three older brothers, which is the kiss of death itself. Then there's my mother, who is from the old school, and believes a daughter should be raised to be a proper wife and hostess to her husband. She was horrified when I went to college to get my degree, and I know my father was disappointed, too."

Austin's hand rubbed small soothing circles at the base of her spine, and he could feel the rasp of her silky stockings against his slacks. He ignored the flash of heat that touched off a deep, inexplicable hunger for her, and steered his concentration back to their conversation. "Why can't you do both, have a successful career and be a wife? Women do it all the time."

A wry look crossed her features. "The two don't seem to mix well for me. Remember Bartholomew? Well, I almost did the deed with him, and luckily came to my senses before I became a clone of my mother. That's another incident my parents have yet to forgive me for." Her gaze conveyed an unmistakable reckless defiance. "I'm not ready to settle down yet. I've got goals to attain, and quite frankly, after being stifled for more years than I care to recall, I like my freedom and independence."

"Maybe you just haven't found the right man yet."

"I'm not looking for a man, remember." With a sassy grin, she reminded him of that vow with a wave of her left hand in front of his face. That sparkly ring of hers flashed, backing her claim. "Staying single is so much easier and less complicated."

"But a lot lonelier." His voice was quiet, but his words were powerful enough to touch the vulnerability behind her independent facade.

Their gazes connected, hers filled with unspoken affirmation. Even though he knew she'd never admit to being lonely, he suspected that the world she'd created for herself didn't keep her warm at night, or bolster her spirits on a bad day. What she needed was someone who believed in her and her aspirations, someone who supported her unconditionally, and didn't try to clip her wings.

It was clear to him that she was out to prove something to her parents, and herself. And possibly even to Louden. He didn't begrudge her the success she strove for, only hoped that her single-mindedness didn't keep her from enjoying other aspects of her life.

"I suppose you want a wife, kids, and the whole bit," she said cheekily, avoiding the deeper issue he'd unintentionally provoked.

"Sure I do." And the older he got, the more he wanted that kind of security. That big Victorian he lived in by himself got far too quiet at night, giving him too much time to think about how a special woman might fit into his life. Finding her was another matter, especially when Fantasy for Hire robbed him of any spare time. "When the right woman comes along, I've got an open mind about marriage. And I want a big family, too. I love kids."

She gave a shudder, but he knew she was exaggerating by the teasing sparkle in her eyes. "I get my fill of kids with my eight nieces and nephews. One night with them, and I'm completely wiped out."

He lifted an eyebrow, wondering how much of that statement was truth, and how much she'd tried to convince herself of.

The final song ended, bringing the Christmas party to a close. Slowly, reluctantly, he let her move from his embrace. A sense of loss filled him—there were no more excuses to postpone the end of the evening. And judging by the slant of their conversation, he pretty much ascertained that no further invitation was forthcoming from her lips to see him again.

She'd made it clear that her job was her priority, that a real man in her life was something her parents wanted, but she had no time or desire for. He wasn't going to push the issue...at least not much.

On the drive back to Teddy's place, Austin had plenty of time to mentally plan his strategy to sway Teddy into giving them another chance, another date, one that wasn't tangled up with lies and pretenses. Just them. And their attraction for one another.

He wondered if he stood a chance against her restricting goals, wondered if he was being foolish for wanting to pursue something that might be all one-sided. And then there was the issue of her family, and what they expected of Teddy...and of a boyfriend.

Meeting their expectations would be impossible, but at the moment none of that mattered to Austin, not when his chest ached at the thought of never seeing Teddy again.

Not when he wanted this woman so badly that physical need coalesced with strong emotion.

After parking the Mustang at the curb, he insisted on walking Teddy to her condo. She wrapped the shawl around her in an attempt to chase away the midnight chill, but her teeth began to chatter. Slipping his tuxedo jacket off, he draped it over her shoulders, and she snuggled into the warmth.

She smiled up at him. "Thanks." Her voice held a slight quiver, but he wasn't sure if it was from the cold, or if she was nervous.

"I had a great time tonight." He'd especially enjoyed their elevator ride up, and slow dancing with her—both opportunities had been private, and incredibly enlightening.

She rolled her eyes. "Between Louden, and Janet, it was certainly interesting, if anything."

He smiled. "I think everything went well. We established a believable relationship, so hopefully Louden will back off like you hope."

She held up crossed fingers for luck. "As long as Janet doesn't remember you as a cop who strips, we'll be in good shape."

Taking the house key from her grasp, he unlocked the door and opened it for her. She handed him back his jacket, started to step inside, then turned around before she cleared the threshold. A light from the living room behind her illuminated her slender form and tipped her upswept hair with gold. Even in the shadows, her eyes shimmered with regret.

"Well, I guess this is goodbye," she said softly, and offered him a slight smile.

The last thing he wanted to say was goodbye. "Not just yet."

Reaching into the pocket of the tuxedo jacket draped over his arm, he withdrew the sprig of mistletoe he'd swiped off their table as they'd left the party. The greenery was crushed, but still in working order. Her rich, chocolate brown eyes widened as he braced his arm on the doorjamb and dangled the mistletoe above her head.

His stance was lazy, deceptively so, and he grinned wickedly, declaring his intent. "I believe you and I have unfinished business to attend to."

6

SHE SHOULD HAVE said no. She should have resisted. But Teddy didn't stand a chance against the seductive pull of Austin's darkened gaze, or the knowledge that this man made her feel restless, needy sensations no other man had ever evoked.

Reckless desire caused her pulse to race. The promise of pleasure glimmering in his sexy eyes touched off a quiver of anticipation deep in her belly. And because she knew he'd make good on that silent vow, she impetuously decided that one last, parting kiss to remember him by wouldn't hurt anything.

His warm fingers brushed along her jaw and curled around the nape of her neck, urging her to meet him halfway, persuading her to participate and give as much as she took. She swayed toward him, too eager to taste him, too anxious to experience the heady thrill of having his mouth on hers.

His head lowered, hers raised expectantly. His lashes fell slumberously, she closed her eyes and waited. His mouth skimmed hers gently, teasing her unmercifully. Her lips parted with a soft, inviting sigh, and he gradually deepened the kiss, slowly, seductively, cajoling her tongue to mate with his, and offering his own in return.

The kiss was incredibly erotic, a lazy, tantalizing possession of the senses. It inflamed and stimulated a depthless passion, and there was nothing she could do but surrender.

Abandoning all coherent thought, all common sense, she tossed her small purse somewhere behind her in the condo, twined her fingers into the thick strands of hair at the back of his neck and opened her mouth wider beneath his and whimpered, a silent plea for him to ease the ache building within her.

He answered with a deep, dark growl that reverberated in his throat, and with her face framed between his palms and her mouth anchored firmly beneath his, he guided her backward, into the darkened entryway, kicking the door shut behind them. A cool whoosh of air caressed her stockinged legs as he dropped his coat at their feet. Pushing her against the wall, he dragged the shawl from her shoulders to join his jacket, and pressed his hard, muscular body against hers, the urgency in him undeniable. Her knees threatened to buckle, but he wedged a leg between her thighs, and she felt the swell of his erection against her belly—thick, hot and pulsing. The male heat of him surrounded her, engulfed her, sparking a liquid fire that settled low in her stomach.

His breathing roughened, and his heart hammered as frantically as her own. She identified with that out-of-control need, and it frightened her as much as it thrilled her. Her head spun, her mind whirled, and the crazy momentum didn't show any signs of slowing.

He continued to kiss her, wild, greedy, insatiable kisses she returned with an enthusiasm that should have shocked her, but didn't. Like a thief, he pilfered and ravished. Like a willing captive, she succumbed and yearned for more.

He obliged her, sliding his fingers into her hair and gently dislodging the rhinestone pins securing the strands. He found each clip, untangled each one and dropped them to the carpeted floor until her hair tumbled around her shoulders in a tousled mess. He crushed the silky tresses in his hands, massaging her scalp, her nape, and then her shoulders.

Finally, he freed her lips, and she moaned as he touched his open mouth to her throat, stroking his soft tongue across the pulse point at the base. And then he bit her sensitive skin, gently, just enough to cause another rush of excitement. She was so distracted by this new, delicious sensation that she was unaware of him slipping his thumbs beneath the thin straps of her dress and dragging them down her arms until she felt the fabric covering her breasts give way.

She gasped at the shock of cool air against her heated skin, felt her first bout of modesty as he lifted his head and looked his fill. His eyes burned with hunger, his gaze ravaged. She shivered, but didn't move. Nor did she protest when he licked the tips of his fingers and slicked them over her nipples, drawing them into tight, aching points. But she groaned, long and low, when he lowered his mouth and laved those tender crests with his tongue, then drew her into the hot depths of his mouth.

Biting her lower lip to keep from crying out, she pushed her fingers into his hair, brazenly holding him close as he leisurely lapped and suckled and nuzzled. He worked his wet mouth from one breast to the other, his tongue, lips and teeth teasing her with devastating thoroughness. The pleasure was dizzying, and frustrating, and in an attempt to soothe a sharper, more intimate ache, she clamped her thighs against the one riding high between hers and arched into him.

A harsh, aroused sound hissed from Austin, and he buried his face at the side of her neck, his breath hot and moist against her flesh. "Teddy..." he whispered huskily, his voice raw with a want so urgent it invaded every cell of her being. His palms slid down her sides to grip her hips, and rocked her rhythmically against that treacherous thigh of his, building the pressure. "All night I've thought about the taste of you, the feel of you. It's not enough. Not nearly enough."

Passion fogged her mind, short-circuiting rational thought. "Not enough," she echoed the sentiment, turning her head to the side to give him better access to the column of her throat.

His tongue touched the delicate shell of her ear, making her skin quiver, and his hands roamed lower, beneath the hem of her dress. Questing fingers rasped against the stockings covering her legs, her thighs...higher still. "I want to make love to you."

Yes, her body screamed, her feminine nerves already spiraling toward that release. All it would take to send her over the edge was the touch of his fingers against slick folds of flesh, the seductive caress of his mouth on her breasts. The elemental need to make love to this man mixed with something deep and soul-stirring, overwhelming her with emotions she'd severed herself from years ago.

Panicked that he could make her feel so much when she'd been content to be alone, she pressed her palms to his chest, pushing gently, but firmly. "Austin, we can't do this."

He immediately stopped his seduction, slowly withdrawing his hand from beneath her dress, leaving her aroused, and very disappointed. The rhinestone straps of her dress slid back up, and the bodice covered her breasts once again.

Concern etched his features, and he brushed her hair away from her face, his gaze searching. "Hey, you okay?"

No. She was scared, and confused, but admitting either defeated the purpose of all those years she'd struggled to build her confidence. "This is happening too fast."

"We can take it slow," he said, his deep, rich voice still holding the vestiges of desire. Bracing an arm against the wall at the side of her head, he skimmed his knuckles down her cheek in a feather-light caress. "As slow and easy as you need it to be."

Her skin tingled at the thought of how good slow could be with this sexy fantasy man. "Impossible, when I unravel when you just look at me, and I melt when you touch me." Like now, those insidious fingers of his were causing all kinds of havoc with her libido.

A roguish grin curved his mouth, and he looked pleased with that revelation. "No, slow doesn't seem to apply to the attraction between us," he agreed. "But I'm not just talking about sex, Teddy. I'm talking about us."

She swallowed, hard, trying to keep her rising wariness at bay. "Us?"

"Yeah," he murmured, trailing that treacherous finger along her jaw to her lobe, eliciting a deep, dark shiver that made her body feel like warm molasses. "You. Me. A slow building relationship. *Us.*"

She shook her head, feeling crowded, and not just because his body surrounded hers. Emotionally, he was slipping under her skin, forcing her to reevaluate her personal life, and she didn't care for what she was discovering. Moving around him, she put some distance between them, shoring up her fortitude. "There is no 'us.'"

"There could be." When she didn't respond, the set of his jaw turned determined. "You honestly believe there isn't something between us worth pursuing?"

She rubbed the slow throb beginning in her temples, and chose her words carefully. "I can't afford any diversions right now, Austin." Her voice implored him to understand. "Not when I'm so close to getting everything I've worked so hard for. And I can't allow great sexual chemistry to distract me when I need to stay focused on my job." She'd only wanted a date for the evening, her own personal fantasy for hire. When had things become so complicated? "Besides, you and I have different goals, and certainly opposite visions of the future."

"Not as much as you might think," he said, ruthless intent in his gaze. "Or maybe it's just easier for you to believe that."

Anger flared within her, that he'd touched on part of the truth—a truth that made her too vulnerable. She was scared of taking personal, emotional risks, for fear of being stifled. It had taken her years to establish her independence, to gain the self-confidence to stand on her own, and there were always those niggling doubts that she couldn't mix business with a relationship and find an equal balance. In her experience, the latter always won.

She grasped a stronger argument. "You fulfill women's fantasies, for crying out loud! How opposite is that?"

He jammed his hands on his lean hips and sighed, sounding as weary as he was beginning to look. "It's just a job, Teddy, and it isn't who I am. Fantasy for Hire was a means to an end. It isn't my entire life."

There was more. She could see it in his eyes. But she didn't want to hear anything else, didn't want to give him a chance to sway her decision. "As much as I want you, I can't do this right now. I don't have time in my life for a relationship, and that's not fair to you."

He stepped toward her, so genuine and understanding. "Teddy—"

She held up a hand to stop him, knowing his touch to be a powerful persuasion. "Please, Austin," she beseeched him. "Don't make this any more difficult than it already is. You're a great guy, and you deserve better than what I can offer you, which is nothing permanent." She bit her bottom lip, acknowledging on some feminine level that she wished she could be the kind of woman he wanted, but she wasn't cut out for marriage, and babies, and all those other things that tied a person down and restricted their freedom.

He stared at her for a long, intense moment, his green eyes darkening with resignation. "All right," he finally relented, and swiped his jacket from the floor. "You win, Teddy."

It wasn't a joyful victory. Her throat burned, and her chest hurt at the thought of never seeing him again. She opened the door before she changed her mind. "Thank you, Austin. For everything."

"The last thing I want is your gratitude for something I *wanted* to do." Just as he passed through the threshold, he stopped and turned back around, his chiseled features expressing deep regret. "Good luck on your promotion, Teddy. I hope you get everything you want."

She was certain the double meaning ringing in his words had been unintentional on his part, but it was there nonetheless, haunting her, forcing her to think about what her desire for that promotion might have cost her. She found the thought disturbing.

And then he was gone, leaving only the warm, male scent of his cologne lingering in the entryway, and a horrible sense of loss blossoming within her.

Leaning against the wall for support, she slid down until she was sitting on the carpeted floor, her knees upraised. Dragging a hand through her tangled hair and trying not to think about how much she enjoyed being with Austin, she let out a deep breath that did nothing to ease the new tension banding her chest.

Her gaze landed on the cluster of mistletoe he'd used to seduce her, and she picked it up, holding the sprig of Christmas spirit in the palm of her hand. Her throat tightened, and a piercing pain wrenched her heart.

Damn Austin McBride anyway, for making her realize just how cold and lonely her life was, for making her question everything that was important to her—everything she'd struggled to attain without the support of anyone.

She'd sacrificed so much to prove her own self-worth to her family, to herself. But this sacrifice was hurting more than she'd ever imagined.

AUSTIN STOOD beneath the hot, stinging spray from the shower. He'd spent a restless night tossing and turning in bed, caused from frustration, confusion and a healthy dose of annoyance that Teddy Spencer had, in effect, brushed him off.

Well, not brushed him off, exactly, he amended as he braced his hands on the tiled wall and dipped his head beneath the invigorating jet of water to rinse his soap-slick body. But her brand of rejection stung nonetheless. He'd served his purpose in aiding Teddy in her plight to dissuade Louden, and she'd never promised him anything beyond last night. He'd *known* that. He'd followed through with Teddy's plan with his eyes wide open, knowing it was all an act. So why did he return home last night with his stomach in knots and a keen sense of disappointment riding him hard?

The answer came easily. Despite knowing Teddy had expected nothing more from him than a performance, he couldn't help feeling used on some basic male level. The unpleasant sensation was one he'd experienced before, and he'd have thought he'd learned from that brief encounter with a woman who'd taken advantage of him for her own self-centered motivations. Diane certainly had her own agenda when she'd pursued him. Too late, he'd discovered that her interest had been for the fantasy he created for her—that of a part-time plaything to keep her occupied when she was bored with her wealthy life and friends. Emotional involvement hadn't been part of her plan—just an exciting affair that abruptly ended when he no longer served a purpose in her capricious life.

Despite that lesson learned, he'd wanted to believe Teddy was different, that her ulterior motives wouldn't cloud what seemed so obvious and right between them.

He'd been wrong.

Swearing at his stupidity, he turned off the water, grabbed the thick navy towel hanging over the stall and scrubbed it over his damp hair and wet body.

"She did you a big favor, buddy," he muttered to himself as he stepped from the shower. "And she's definitely all wrong for you," he continued as he trekked naked into the bedroom, where the early-morning sun was just beginning to seep through the second-story bedroom window to warm the hardwood floor.

Grabbing his favorite pair of soft, faded jeans, he pulled them on and concentrated on all those wrongs, mentally ticking them off in his head: her wealthy family, who wouldn't approve of him, her job being more important than a relationship, and her admitted unwillingness to balance the two.

He finger-combed his thick, damp hair away from his face, and tried not to grimace at the less-than-refreshed reflection in the mirror—he looked tired, haggard and as irritable as a provoked bear. "You have every reason to be grateful that she didn't allow things to progress further than they had last night," he told himself, pivoting toward the bedroom door.

But as he headed downstairs, he found it difficult to be gracious about Teddy's rejection when he'd tasted the need and hunger in her kiss, and in the way her body had responded so openly and honestly to his touch. There had been nothing calculated about her soft groans as he'd caressed her breasts, nothing fabricated about the sensual way she'd arched toward him for more.

Letting out a deep breath to erase those arousing thoughts that would surely haunt him for months to come, he entered the kitchen. Jordan, who'd always been one to be up bright and early, flipped down the corner of the Sunday sports section and glanced at Austin. A slow grin spread across Jordan's face as he homed in on his brother's cantankerous disposition.

"You look like hell this morning, little brother." Humor threaded Jordan's voice and creased the corners of his eyes.

Austin gave a noncommittal grunt in response. Of course, Jordan looked neat and orderly and ready to begin the day, his knit shirt pressed, and his jeans crisp and a vivid shade of blue, which indicated they were fairly new. Austin barely contained a disgusted snort. Didn't his brother ever dress for anything but success?

Jordan's grin increased. "And you should be plenty rested, considering I heard you come in just a little after midnight."

Jordan's insinuation that Austin's evening plans hadn't ended as he'd personally hoped rankled. Crossing the cool tiled floor, he opened the cupboard and brought down a bowl and a box of cereal, then withdrew a carton of milk from the refrigerator. "I thought I'd outgrown you waiting up for me long ago."

"Oh, I wasn't waiting up." Jordan folded the section of newspaper neatly, and laid it aside. "I was awake, in bed reading. Even if I wasn't, the way you stomped up the stairs and slammed your bedroom door would have woken the dead."

He grimaced as he carried his breakfast items to the table. "Sorry," he said, genuinely contrite. Sitting across from Jordan, he poured Cap'n Crunch into his bowl and added a generous amount of milk. Jordan looked on disapprovingly at the sugared cereal, which Austin had eaten for breakfast since the age of eight.

Jordan believed in a healthy start to the day; Austin wasn't about to sacrifice his favorite cereal for the scrambled eggs, wheat toast and cantaloupe his brother preferred. "I guess I'm still not used to having someone else in the house."

"I figured as much." Jordan shoveled scrambled eggs onto his buttered wheat toast and took a bite while considering Austin through curious eyes. "Dare I ask how things went last night?"

Austin tried for a nonchalant shrug and failed miserably. "Depends on whose point of view you want."

"How about hers?" Jordan asked, slicing his cantaloupe into precise wedges.

"Great." Unequivocally, Austin was sure. There was little doubt in his mind that everyone at Sharper Image had fallen for the ruse, which could only work to Teddy's favor.

"And yours?"

He scooped up a spoonful of cereal, glancing at Jordan before taking the bite. "Disappointing and frustrating."

And a multitude of other emotions he didn't care to verbally analyze.

Jordan digested that, appearing sympathetic. "Care to talk about it?"

Austin wasn't one to spill his guts about personal issues, but Jordan had always been a good listener, reflective without judging, and Austin needed that quiet male camaraderie and support right now. "The night itself was great. In fact, I can't remember the last time I had such a good time with a woman. Teddy is smart, sexy, amusing...and entirely too determined," he added on a note of annoyance.

Jordan lifted an eyebrow. "Usually that's a good thing."

Austin pushed his half-eaten bowl of Cap'n Crunch aside. "She's determined to the point of seeing nothing beyond her promotion."

"Can't begrudge a person for wanting to be successful."

Austin didn't miss the bitter note to his brother's voice that had nothing to do with Teddy.

"I don't begrudge Teddy for wanting that promotion, but what about being successful *and* making time for a relationship?"

Jordan picked up his glass of orange juice. "Depends on the person's priorities."

Austin snorted. Teddy had made it patently clear where her priorities lay—in the hands of Sharper Image. "I guess I went with her to this party expecting something...different. Like maybe another date, where we could get to know one another without that ridiculous charade between us." Shaking his head, he scrubbed a hand over the light stubble covering his jaw. "Man, it's been a long time since I've felt that way about a woman."

Jordan chuckled, the sound entirely too gleeful. "She certainly has you tied up in knots."

Austin scowled, but knew he'd be a hypocrite if he denied what was so obviously the truth. Teddy did have a hold on him, one he couldn't shake. She made him think about things he'd decided were beyond his reach until his landscaping business was financially stable. She made him think about what it would be like to come home to her smiles in the evening and her soft, feminine scent filling this old Victorian house. And then there was the luxury of making love to her every night, and waking up beside her for the next fifty years.

Commitment. Security. And the comfort of having a family. After years of playing the field, the notion appealed to him. More and more with each passing year.

Folding his hands over his bare belly, Austin leaned back in his chair, rocking on the solid hind legs. "Jordan, you ever think about settling down?"

Stacking his fork and knife on his plate, Jordan shrugged noncommittally. "I thought I was close once, but it didn't work out, which is just as well because look at where I am now. If I had a family to support, I never would have been able to quit and walk out on those dishonest bastards."

Austin nodded in understanding.

"Now, I'm an unemployed architect, living with my bachelor brother, and I have no idea what the future holds."

"You could always take over Fantasy for Hire," Austin offered with a devilish grin.

Jordan visibly shuddered. "I'm nobody's fantasy, and I prefer to conduct business with my clothes *on*, thank you very much."

"You don't give yourself near enough credit. I'm sure

there are women out there who fantasize about straitlaced architects." Austin ignored the dirty look Jordan cast his way. "I'd sell you the business real cheap."

"What, you thinking of giving up being the object of every woman's fantasy?" Humor threaded through Jordan's voice.

"I've been considering selling the business for a while now," Austin admitted. "Not only is Fantasy for Hire becoming too much for me to handle along with all the business coming in for McBride Landscaping, I'm tired of all the pretense."

"Feeling a little taken advantage of, hmm?"

He hadn't, not until he'd met Teddy. For this particular reason, he'd always been careful to draw the line between his job as a fantasy for hire and the customer he performed for, but that's where he'd failed with Teddy Spencer. He'd brazenly stepped over that line because of an intense, mind-boggling attraction, and he'd gotten burned for his efforts.

Teddy would rather cling to the fantasy than grasp the reality of what was between them.

"I want a normal life," Austin said, hearing the frustration in his own voice. "And when I meet a woman, I want to be sure that she's interested in me because of who I am, and not what particular fantasy of hers I might fulfill."

Jordan stood and carried his dishes to the sink, rinsing them. "Sounds like you've got some decisions to make."

"Yeah." He'd already come to the conclusion to put Fantasy for Hire on the market, and after the holidays he'd see if he could find an interested buyer for the business. Then, he'd see what he could do about finding a woman who wanted the *real* Austin McBride.

THE CORDLESS PHONE in Teddy's lap rang, and she tossed aside the woman's magazine she'd been thumbing through and clicked the connect button before the sound completed its cycle.

"Hello?" she answered.

"You are a *very* bad girl, Teddy Spencer."

Teddy immediately recognized her sister-in-law's low, throaty voice. Relief mingled with the awful anxiety that had been her constant companion all day long, easing the knot in her chest by a few degrees. Normally, Sundays were her day to relax and catch up on personal errands and chores. Today, she'd been too intent on talking to Susan to move more than an arm's stretch away from the phone. She hadn't even taken a shower yet because she'd feared missing the call. The only thing she'd allowed for her vigil was a quick change into leggings and an oversize sweatshirt, a scrubbed face, brushed teeth and a ponytail.

Not wanting to appear too anxious, she strove for a casual air. "It's the bad girls that have all the fun."

Susan laughed. "You certainly seem to be having your share," she said, her tone sly. "When were you going to tell the family about Austin? Or were you going to keep this guy all to yourself?"

The latter, but Susan's phone call last night had nixed that plan. Not quite ready to answer that question until she had a chance to feel Susan out, she said, "It's after five. Where have you been? I've been trying to get hold of you all day."

"No kidding." Susan snickered. "Thirteen messages on the answering machine is a bit excessive, don't you think?"

"No." Teddy straightened indignantly. "Not when I needed to speak with you about eight hours ago."

"Brent, the kids and I were out of the house early this morning," Susan said breezily. "We went to brunch with your brother Russ and his family. I would have invited you to come along, but thought you'd have better things to do this morning."

The insinuation in Susan's tone caused Teddy's face to warm and a horrifying thought to invade her mind...the very real possibility that Susan had shared that assumption with her brother Brent. "Susan—"

"Then Brent and Russ took the kids to see that new animated Christmas feature playing at the movies, and me and Natalie went shopping with your mother for Christmas presents for the kids. Santa went broke this year, and what I didn't get on the kids' Christmas list, Grandma insisted on buying."

Teddy shot up off the sofa, her heart slamming against her ribs. Oh, this didn't sound good at all! "You went shopping with my mother?" The question came out as a croak.

"She was on her best behavior," Susan assured her. "I swear, there's something about the holidays that brings out the very best in her. And when I told her about your new guy, she actually beamed."

Teddy squeezed her eyes shut, imagining her mother's pretty face, alight with happiness at the thought that her only daughter was finally coming to her senses and settling down. "No," she moaned.

"Yeah, she actually beamed," Susan reiterated, misinterpreting Teddy's denial. "She looked radiant."

Teddy shook her head, then realized that Susan couldn't see the silent gesture. She didn't know whether to laugh deliriously, or scream at the dreadful turn of events.

All day, her active imagination had come up with various scenarios of how her sister-in-law might have handled last night's conversation with Austin. She'd expected

Susan to mention Austin to Brent, of course, and knew she could have quashed any rumors between the two before they'd circulated through the family. But this...this was her worst nightmare!

"Austin McBride is just a *friend*," she blurted desperately.

"Oh, sure he's just a friend, Teddy," Susan said, clearly expressing her disbelief. "The tiger is out of the bag, honey, and I have to say, he was an incredibly charming, sexy-sounding tiger. The whole family is dying to meet him—"

"The whole family?" she wailed, feeling pushed to the edge of hysteria.

"Of course the whole family. Since he agreed to come for Christmas Eve, I didn't see any reason to keep this exciting news all to myself."

"He *agreed*?" Teddy wheezed, collapsing back onto the sofa. Why hadn't Austin informed her of that minuscule fact? She replayed her conversation with Austin in her mind, and remembered telling him she'd take care of the discussion he'd had with Susan.

"Well, I admit to a teensy-tiny bit of coercion on my part," Susan added impishly.

Teddy rolled her eyes. "You don't know the meaning of subtle."

Susan laughed, as if Teddy had issued her a compliment. When Teddy didn't join in on the humor, Susan attempted to smooth things over. "Honey, I don't know why you're so upset. This is a good thing, really. Your mother is thrilled that you're dating again, especially since this is the first guy we've heard about since Bart."

Just the mention of the fiasco with Bartholomew Winston gave Teddy a migraine.

"And even if Austin *is* just a friend, there is a bright side to all this," Susan offered.

All Teddy saw was doom and gloom in her future. "Which is?"

"Well, I know how particular your parents can be when it comes to who their children date, but I'm thinking that if they see that you're at least making an effort to find a potential husband—not that you are," Susan quickly amended, knowing what a hot button that was for Teddy. "But if your parents believe that, then maybe your mother will leave you alone and quit obsessing about finding you a suitable man."

Teddy rested her head against the back of the sofa and stared up at the ceiling, her instincts rebelling against Susan's preposterous plan. Austin was hardly what her parents would consider "suitable". Yet he'd managed to fool everyone at Sharper Image, her conscience reminded her.

As she mulled over the suggestion, she began to see the merit behind the idea. Introducing Austin to her family didn't mean she had to marry him, for goodness' sake, but showing up with a date would at least pacify her mother into believing her daughter was finally circulating, instead of devoting so much time to "that silly little job" of hers.

Oh, yeah, her mother would be tickled pink. But this grand scheme required seeing Austin again, and that was the tricky part. Not only did the man set off disturbing sensual cravings and make her yearn for things she had no room in her life for, but she was pretty certain she'd chafed that male pride of his with her well-rehearsed speech last night. Which meant she'd be swallowing a large dose of her own pride if she asked this favor of him.

"So, is Austin as scrumptious as he sounds?" Susan asked, her excitement traveling over the phone lines.

Taking a deep breath, she forced a cheerful note to her voice. "You'll have to wait, and see for yourself."

7

TEDDY'S HEAD was killing her. Nearly twenty-four hours after hanging up the phone with Susan, what had started as a slow throbbing in her temples had escalated into full-blown pounding in her skull. Dread was the culprit for her headache. She'd yet to call Austin, and considering Christmas Eve was only a few days away, she knew she couldn't stall the inevitable another day, or even another hour.

Desperate for relief, and wanting her mind calm and focused before she spoke with Austin, she removed her purse from the bottom drawer in her desk and dug for the small bottle of aspirin she carried with her. A loose piece of paper crinkled, and she withdrew the yellow slip, recognizing it as the receipt Austin had given her for the money she'd paid him to escort her to the Christmas party. Except he hadn't accepted her payment, and had instead donated the money to a needy organization. There was nothing to indicate his generous donation on the receipt, but she didn't doubt for a second the sincerity of his claim. Austin was genuine, through and through, and she was about to take advantage of that generosity. Again.

Not wanting her thoughts to travel that road for fear she'd talk herself out of calling him, she tucked the receipt in her desk drawer, right beneath his Fantasy for Hire business card, and continued her search. Finding the plastic bottle, she twisted open the top and shook three tablets into her palm.

Needing water, she headed out of her office, down the plush halls of Sharper Image, to the small, unoccupied kitchenette at the end. Plucking a small paper cup from the dispenser next to the watercooler, she filled it, tossed the pills into her mouth and washed them down in one huge gulp. She closed her eyes, and forced herself to relax, hoping her headache would ebb soon.

Something brushed across her skirt-clad bottom, jolting her back to awareness. Startled, she glanced around and found Louden standing two feet away from her, his pale blue eyes giving nothing away. The caress had been so subtle, she would have thought she'd imagined it if she'd been by herself. She didn't trust Louden, but neither could she prove anything had just happened.

Uneasiness slithered through her. Not wanting to be alone with him, she tossed her paper cup into the trash and turned to leave the kitchenette. He grabbed her arm before she could escape, gently, but firm enough that she couldn't dismiss the gesture.

She glanced sharply at him, and he slowly released his hold, though he remained in her direct path. "I haven't had the chance to ask if you enjoyed the party Saturday night."

He hadn't had the opportunity because she'd deliberately avoided him all day. She'd decided steering clear of Louden as much as possible was the smartest course of action until after next week, when the promotion was either assigned to her, or Fred Williams.

She straightened, meeting his gaze head-on. "The Christmas party was great. Austin and I had a wonderful time."

"Ah, yes, Austin," he murmured reflectively. "What a

surprise it was to finally meet your boyfriend. You two certainly seemed convincing."

Teddy managed a bland smile. "I'm not sure I know what you mean."

"Only that for a man who seemed so attentive during the party, he hasn't shown much devotion otherwise." A smile curved his thin mouth, but didn't reach his eyes. "No flowers on your birthday, no phone calls at work, no lunch dates..."

Teddy shrugged. "He's a busy man."

"I'm sure." He let that insinuation dangle between them as he withdrew a paper cup and filled it with cold water from the cooler. "Care to have a drink with me this evening to discuss the senior graphic design opening?"

In her opinion, there was nothing left to discuss. She qualified for the job in every way that mattered. "No, thank you. I already have other plans." Not caring for the slant of their conversation, she stepped around Louden and headed for the hallway.

"For a woman who wants the position, you're not showing much dedication to Sharper Image."

Teddy immediately stopped, her blood beginning a slow simmer in her veins. Turning, she pinned Louden with a direct look. "My dedication shows in the quality of my work, the deadlines I've never missed and the long hours I put in when necessary."

He sighed, shaking his head regretfully. "But you're not very accommodating when the situation requires it." He took a drink of water, as if he hadn't just issued a double-edged comment.

She forced a calm she was far from feeling. "I don't think Austin would appreciate me meeting with you after hours."

He crushed the paper cup in his hand, as if to prove

how easily he could demolish her dreams. "It's just a drink between colleagues, Teddy. I would think if your boyfriend knew how important this promotion was to you, he'd understand."

Teddy's stomach pitched. After all she'd gone through to establish Austin as her boyfriend, it appeared Louden didn't care that she was committed to someone else.

Crossing her arms over her chest, she smiled sweetly at her boss. "Why don't you see if Fred Williams is able to have a drink with you this evening, and discuss the promotion? Maybe he'll be more accommodating." She turned to leave, but not before she caught a glimpse of Louden's complexion turning an unflattering shade of red.

Feeling wonderfully liberated, she walked back to her office with a light step, shut the door and sat behind her desk. Clinging to that boost of confidence, she picked up the phone, dialed the number for Fantasy for Hire off the business card in her top drawer—the only number she had for Austin—and mentally rehearsed her request while the line rang.

The business recorder clicked on, and as much as she hated leaving a message for Austin when she'd rather talk to him in person, she had no choice. "Hi, Austin, this is Teddy. I'd really like to talk to you—"

The line picked up, interrupting her one-sided conversation. "Hello?"

The voice, though deep and male, wasn't Austin's. Another Fantasy for Hire employee, possibly? "I'm calling for Austin. Is he there?"

"No, he's not, but I can take a message for him."

The voice sounded a bit too eager. "All right," she said, deciding she had no choice. "This is Teddy Spencer. He has my home and work numbers. Tell him I'd really like to talk to him, in person preferably."

"Got it." The friendly voice hesitated a moment, then added, "You know, you're welcome to come by the house and talk to Austin. He should be home in about half an hour."

"The house?" Confusion wove through her. "Isn't this Austin's business?"

"One and the same," he confirmed. "He runs Fantasy for Hire out of the house."

"Oh." She imagined a dozen males in Austin's house, dressed in various sexy costumes as they consulted their schedules for fantasy appointments. Doubt filled her— maybe going to Austin's house wasn't such a great idea. "Uh, I don't think I should infringe on Austin's business time—"

"You wouldn't be," he assured her. "This is Austin's brother, Jordan," the male voice went on to explain. "He's told me about you, Teddy. I'm sure he wouldn't mind if you stopped by to see him."

She had to trust that Jordan knew Austin well enough to make such a statement. "Okay." She jotted down the address Jordan gave her. "I'll be there in an hour."

"Great," he said effusively. "I can't wait to meet you."

Teddy hung up the phone, hoping Austin shared his brother's enthusiasm about her surprise visit.

"YOU DID WHAT?" Austin glared at his meddlesome brother.

Jordan held his hands up in a supplicating gesture. "Hey, she said she needed to talk to you in person. It sounded important, and I'm not one to turn down a woman in distress."

"Distress?" Austin laughed dryly at Jordan's description. "Teddy can take care of herself just fine. Whatever she needed to talk to me about could have been done over the phone." He would have preferred that, actually. The past two days, he hadn't been able to think about anything but her. One date, if he could even term escorting her to her Christmas party as such, and she had his hormones and emotions twisted into something he refused to examine. Seeing her in person again, being close enough to touch her, was going to kill him.

And what in the world could be so important that she had to talk to him in person?

"Regardless, she'll be here any minute," Jordan said, then frowned at Austin. "And you look like you've been digging ditches all day."

"Pretty damn close." He'd been shorthanded today on the landscaping project under development for a newly built condominium complex and had spent the afternoon helping his guys install an elaborate sprinkler system, along with planting trees, shrubs and ground cover. Digging ditches wasn't beneath him, not in his chosen profession.

Jordan waved an impatient hand toward the upper facilities. "I suggest you go and take a shower before she gets here."

Austin glanced down at himself, a slow grin pulling up the corners of his mouth. He'd taken off his dirt-encrusted work boots at the back door leading into the kitchen, but the rest of his attire was just as filthy. A combination of soil and sweat coated his skin and adhered to his T-shirt and jeans. Dust layered his thick hair. Hell, he could even taste the day's grime in his mouth. He was half tempted to greet Teddy just as he was, to give her a good look at what her investment broker looked like at the end of a workday.

"Well?" Jordan prompted, wrinkling his nose at him. "Time's a ticking, and the longer you stand here, the more Glade freshener I'm going to have to use to cover up that outdoorsy scent of yours."

Austin spouted an obscene gesture that made Jordan's mouth twitch with amusement. "Since you invited her over, you can entertain her until I'm cleaned up," Austin said, none too happy about the situation.

"Hey, I thought I was doing you a favor," Jordan called after him as he climbed the stairs to his room.

"Yeah, well, next time, *don't*," Austin said over his shoulder.

He heard Jordan mutter something about what an ungrateful brother he was, and took it all in stride. Heading into the bathroom, he peeled his dirty shirt over his head, tossed it into the hamper, then removed his jeans. By the time he exited the shower fifteen minutes later and pulled on a pair of cutoff shorts and a clean T-shirt, he could hear Teddy's voice drifting from downstairs. He headed in that direction, following the sounds to the living room, where Jordan and Teddy were standing near the potted Douglas fir he'd brought home a week ago. He'd retrieved the small box of Christmas ornaments from the attic last night and placed it next to the tree, but hadn't had the chance to decorate it yet.

Not quite ready to make his presence known, Austin leaned against the door frame and crossed his arms over his chest, watching the two of them interact.

Jordan scratched his chin, a disapproving expression on his face. "I tried telling Austin that the tree was a bit on the piteous side, but he seems to think a string of garland will spruce it up."

Tucking her silky blond hair behind her ear, Teddy tilted her head, a soft smile on her face as she scrutinized the tree. "Oh, I don't know. I think the tree has potential. Garland might overpower the branches, but maybe we could find something in this box to liven it up without weighing it down." She glanced at Jordan hesitantly. "Would you mind if I gave it a shot while we're waiting for Austin?"

A too-cheerful smile curved Jordan's mouth. "By all means, help yourself."

Traitor, Austin thought with a dark scowl. He opened his mouth to announce his presence, then snapped it shut when Teddy bent over to rummage through the box of decorative items, which pulled her skirt taut over her bottom and lifted the hem a few inches. Man, oh, man, the woman had a fine backside, not to mention a pair of long, slender legs that inspired erotic thoughts. Images flitted through his mind, of coming up behind her and skimming his hands over her slim hips and pressing his hard body to hers...of her widening her stance as he shimmed up her skirt, caressing her firm thighs...

She straightened abruptly, flashing a spool of red ribbon Jordan's way. "What do you think about this velvet ribbon?"

Austin liked the idea of velvet ribbon, a whole lot...especially if those possibilities included mutual, pleasurable bondage and erotic explorations...

"I could make some small bows to tie around the branches," she suggested, her face radiant and her eyes sparkling with excitement. "And here's a piece of green velvet we can use around the base."

Jordan withdrew a pair of scissors from the Queen Anne desk next to him and handed the shears to Teddy. "Perfect."

Yeah, she was perfect, Austin thought. Beautiful, smart,

a fabulous kisser, fun to be with...and she didn't want anything to do with him, he sternly reminded himself.

Teddy snipped a section of red ribbon and twisted it into a pretty bow. "It's been years since I've decorated a tree," she said, a touch of melancholy in her voice.

Jordan cast her a sideways glance as he took over the job of cutting sections of ribbon for her to tie. "Your parents don't get a tree at Christmas?" He sounded as curious as Austin was.

"Oh, they do, usually a twelve-foot blue spruce. But my mother hires a professional to decorate the tree so the trim and ornaments match with the house and look evenly distributed on the branches." She added another bow, swaddled the green velvet around the base to cover the plastic pot, then stepped back to admire her handiwork. "When I was a child, my mother used to let me hang a few of the decorations just to appease me, but by the next day my ornaments were either gone, or rearranged on the tree."

"That must have been tough," Jordan commented insightfully.

Austin didn't want to care about Teddy and her *underprivileged* youth, yet something near the vicinity of his heart tugged for the little girl Teddy had been, and how she'd been denied one of Christmas's favorite rituals enjoyed by most kids. He could easily picture her as a mischievous little girl, full of energy and curiosity.

Teddy shrugged, as if having come to terms with her mother's peculiarities long ago. "Now that I live alone, buying a tree and decorating it seems like so much work, especially when I don't have anyone to share it with."

For as much as she declared the importance of embracing her freedom, Austin heard the note of loneliness in her voice, and wondered how much of her need for independence was pure rebellion. Ninety percent of it, he'd bet.

Finished with the last of the bows, she rummaged through the box and withdrew an old, fond memory of Austin's. A dazzling smile lit her face. "This papier-mâché star is great!"

A wry smile curved Jordan's mouth. "Austin made that for our mother for Christmas when he was in the seventh grade. She loved it and used it every year until she died."

Teddy touched the handmade ornament reverently. There was nothing special or fancy about the star—it was just a hodgepodge of paper, glitter and yarn a twelve year old boy had glued together—but Austin imagined Teddy silently wished her own mother would have been so accepting of a gift handcrafted with youthful love and enthusiasm.

She glanced back at Jordan. "It's the perfect decoration to top the tree, wouldn't you agree?"

Her softly spoken question asked Jordan's permission to adorn the Douglas fir with Austin's star. He nodded. "Yeah, I do."

Austin steeled himself against the rush of feeling that stirred to life within him. This scene was too cozy, a false illusion when he knew Teddy would never allow those emotional needs he'd glimpsed in the past few minutes to interfere with her personal goals.

That sobering thought prompted him to push off the doorjamb and fully enter the room, startling both Jordan and Teddy. His brother looked at him questioningly, while an anxious look flitted across Teddy's expression. She wiped her palms down the sides of her skirt, making him wonder why she'd sought him out again when she'd made it abundantly clear she didn't have time in her life for a relationship. Or for him.

Another business proposition, he guessed. The thought

rubbed him raw, but he couldn't help being curious. Neither could he help wanting her as badly as he did.

Man, she did have him tied up in knots.

He closed the distance between them, catching the awareness glittering in her gaze, the flutter of her pulse at the base of her throat and the slight quiver of her breasts beneath the dark green, silk blouse she wore. The satisfaction he experienced was heady.

"I see you've met my brother," he drawled, smiling pleasantly.

"I, uh, yes," she stammered, a nervous smile on her lips. "We were just trying to make your tree a bit more presentable for Santa."

His gaze flickered to the ugly duckling of a tree she'd transformed into a swan, then back to her. "As much as I'm sure Santa will appreciate your efforts, I'm certain you didn't drop by to make sure I had a well-decorated tree for the holidays."

Jordan frowned at his brother's cool tone. But in Austin's mind, even though their mother had taught them to be gentlemen, there was the matter of his ego being bruised.

"No, I didn't," she admitted, that chin of hers lifting a notch. "I'd like to talk to you. Privately, if that's okay."

He stared into her unwavering brown eyes, tempted beyond all reason. For all of three seconds he considered telling her no, that whatever was on her mind could be said in front of Jordan, but he wasn't that much of a cad. Besides, he really didn't care to share this conversation with his brother.

"Private it is," he said. "Why don't we step into my office."

"Behave yourself," Jordan muttered beneath his breath. Austin glared at his brother's protective gesture toward

Teddy before heading toward the back room. Geez, whose side was Jordan on, anyway?

Teddy watched Austin go, suddenly doubting the wisdom of her visit. Austin was hardly welcoming, nor did he seem inclined to accommodate yet another request of hers.

A gentle hand nudged her. "Go on," Jordan murmured from beside her. "He's all bark and no bite."

Encouraged by Jordan's support, she smiled her thanks and followed the sexy, moody man she couldn't get out of her mind through a door that connected to a kitchen, where he stopped to grab a can of root beer from the refrigerator. Popping the top, he offered her a drink of her own that she declined, and they continued, to another room transformed into a makeshift office. He closed the door behind her, and her heart leaped in response to just how alone they were.

There were no chairs other than the one behind the scarred desk dominating the room, so she advanced no farther. The phone rang at that moment, and Austin rounded the desk, propped his jean-clad hip on the surface and reached for the receiver.

"Fantasy for Hire," he greeted the caller.

Teddy tried not to let that deep, rich voice of his affect her, but her attempts were futile. The warm male tones stroked her senses and settled in the pit of her stomach like a potent shot of liquor.

"Hi, Don," Austin said after a moment, and turned to flip through the schedule open on the desk. His index finger scanned down a page, then stopped. "I've got you lined up for two fantasies tonight. A fireman at seven-thirty, and Zorro at ten."

Teddy listened to the conversation with some amusement as she glanced around the cluttered office, trying not to think about Austin performing his share of fantasies for countless women. In her attempt to keep her mind occupied, her gaze was inevitably drawn to his wide, muscled shoulders stretching the cotton of his T-shirt, then moved to his profile, and eventually stopped on those incredible lips of his.

He grinned at something the caller said. "Hey, you're the one who thought up the Zorro costume, and it's become a favorite. Just be careful with that sword of yours." Austin chuckled at the other man's response, which Teddy didn't doubt was a bawdy one.

Excusing himself from the conversation for a moment, Austin covered the mouthpiece with his hand, his gaze on her. "C'mere and sit down, Teddy." With his bare foot, he pushed the rolling high-backed chair out a few inches from where he sat. "I'll be done in a minute."

To refuse would make her look uptight, so she sat down and waited while Austin gave his employee directions to each performance. He hung up the phone, then turned those sexy, intense green eyes on her.

"So, what can I do for you, Ms. Spencer?" Picking up his root beer, he took a long swallow while he waited for her to answer.

She crossed one leg over the other, taking a second to gather her courage. "I need to ask a favor."

The faintest hint of a smile tipped his mouth. "Another fantasy?"

Seeing the spark of insolence in his eyes, she knew he wasn't going to make this conversation easy on her, not that she blamed him after the way they'd parted Saturday night. There was no way to sugarcoat her request, so she just came out with it. "No, I was hoping you would come with me to my parents' house Christmas Eve."

Surprise crossed his gorgeous features. "Now, why would I want to do that?"

Yes, *why?* her conscience taunted. "Because you promised my sister-in-law that you would, and she told the rest of the family you'd be there."

He finished his root beer, appearing unconcerned. "Your sister-in-law made assumptions, and you were supposed to clear them up."

Frustration nipped at her. "I did." At least she'd tried to, not that it had worked.

"Another charade?" he guessed, his mouth thinning in disdain.

Her entire life was beginning to feel like one big scheme—at work, with her family. Everything was a carefully orchestrated plan...except for her feelings for Austin, which were too real, and becoming more complicated than she'd ever expected. "No, not another charade," she told him. "I explained that you were just a friend."

He tensed, the muscles across his chest flexing with the movement. "How convenient."

She closed her eyes, hating his contempt, but taking full responsibility for his resentment. Lifting her lashes, she met his dark, penetrating gaze, inwardly admitting defeat. "You know what, I think coming here was a big mistake."

She stood to leave, but he was faster, moving like a lithe panther. Propping his bare feet on either side of her thighs, he reeled the chair in closer to him with the strength of his legs, jarring her back into her seat. He leaned forward, looming over her. His strong, powerful thighs were close enough to touch...and so was that solid chest of his. Trapped between the chair and two hundred pounds of pure male essence and heat, her heart fluttered uncontrollably...with shameless excitement, and apprehension.

"What do you *really* want from me this time, Teddy?" he asked, his tone low and rough. "I gave you a cowboy. I gave you a lover. What fantasy do you expect me to be now?"

The frustrated undertone to his voice perplexed her, as did this issue he had with being a fantasy for her. "I don't want you to be any fantasy. I want you to be...a friend. I could really use a friend right now." Between the pressures of her family, and Louden's strong-arm tactics, she desperately needed someone in her corner.

Something in his expression softened, then was quickly replaced with ruthless intent. "That poses a little problem, honey, because when I look at you, friendship isn't what comes to mind."

Yeah, Teddy, why would he want to be your friend after the way you treated him? To her consternation, her throat tightened and a suspicious moisture burned the backs of her eyes. "I know you probably hate me for how I ended things Saturday night—"

"Hate you?" Harsh, incredulous laughter erupted from him. "No, I don't hate you, Teddy. I *want* you." He stared at her face, and slowly lifted his hand, tracing a finger along her jaw. "I haven't slept the past few nights because every time I close my eyes I think of you and remember the heat and softness of your mouth..." He stroked his thumb along her full bottom lip, dipping just inside to dampen the pad of his finger. "The silky texture of your skin..." Those sensual fingers skimmed down her throat in a languid caress that made her breathing raspy, and caused her chest to rise and fall rapidly. "The warm taste of your breasts..." He brushed his knuckles over the slope of those swelling mounds, teasing her nipples into hard, achy points.

And just like that, her body hummed with arousal and an excruciating need.

He lifted his slumberous gaze from her breasts. One look into those striking green eyes filled with steely determination and she knew he wasn't done tormenting her.

A wicked smile lifted his lips. "And if that isn't enough to drive me crazy, I imagine what it would feel like to be inside you, as deep as I can get, and hear my name on your lips when you come..."

A surge of liquid warmth pooled in her belly, and lower. Her mind spun dizzily. "Austin..." she moaned raggedly.

"Yeah, just like that, Teddy." His voice vibrated with husky gratification, and he moved back slightly. His eyes, however, had no qualms about seducing her. "I'm not even inside you, not even touching you as intimately as I'd like to, but just thinking about having your legs wrapped around my hips and making love to you makes me hard enough to go off like an untried teenager."

She had a clear view of just how hard and impressive that part of his anatomy was beneath the faded denim of his shorts. Swallowing the thickness gathering in her throat, she pressed her knees together in a valiant attempt to ease the throbbing need he'd cleverly ignited. The attempt was useless.

Her gaze traveled upward, to his face. "So, you really don't hate me?" For some reason, having him confirm that was important to her.

He shook his head, his gaze honest. "No, I don't hate you, Teddy. I think you're nervous about what you feel for me and how fast our attraction has grown...and where it might lead."

She bit the inside of her cheek, unwilling to admit how accurate he was. She'd never planned for this, for him, and she feared she'd never be able to balance a career, and relationship—and that ultimately, she'd have to choose between the two.

"Then will you come with me to my parents' on Christmas Eve?" This time, she wasn't talking about a business arrangement. She wanted him to accompany her, and be a part of that special, magical evening before Christmas— and hopefully, his presence would banish the loneliness that always threatened to overwhelm her when she left her parents and realized that she was the only one in the family who didn't have anyone to share the holidays with.

Pure Christmas melancholy, she knew, but the desolate feeling never failed to creep up on her and hang on through the first of the year. Maybe this year would be different.

"If I say yes, I don't want any pretenses between us this time," Austin said, clasping his hands loosely between his knees so that he was no longer touching her. "Just you, and me, and whatever happens from there. And if all this leads to just friendship, then I'll accept that."

She found his terms more than fair. "All right."

A devastatingly charming grin transformed his features. "You brave enough to put your promise where your mouth is?"

She swallowed hard, knowing she was playing with fire...but she found Austin's brand of virile heat impossible to resist. The dare in his eyes spurred the recklessness she tried to keep buried.

Dampening her bottom lip with her tongue, she reached out, curled her fingers into the material of his shirt and pulled him down for a kiss the same time she sat up and met him halfway. Her lips crushed his, parted with immediate warmth, skipping all preliminary foreplay and going straight to the heart of the matter. The kiss was a hot, lusty, tongue-tangling mission to drive him as wild as he made her.

But something changed during the course of her provocative goal—an internal realization that overrode the pleasure of his generous mouth surrendering to her whims. She'd missed him. Two days apart, and she longed to see that wicked glint in his eyes, ached to experience the special way he made her feel, and especially craved the effortless way he made her body, her soul, come alive.

It was a frightening, overwhelming sensation.

With a low growl that rumbled in his chest, he grasped her hips in his hands, pulling her up and out of the chair and between his thighs. His large palms smoothed over her bottom, anchoring her intimately close. Her belly encountered the stiff ridge of his erection, and her heart slammed against her ribs. She moaned into his mouth as a very urgent, naughty thought crossed her mind, of pressing him down on his desk, hiking up her skirt and finishing what he'd started with his erotic monologue a few minutes ago.

It was Austin who ended the embrace, slowly pulling back and letting his lips slide from her mouth, to her jaw. "Oh, yeah, Ms. Spencer," he growled into the curve of her neck, where he nuzzled and pressed damp, open-mouth kisses on her skin. "That's a fantastic start to making good on your promise."

A delicious shiver rippled down her spine and she stepped back, until he had no choice but to let her go. Meeting his fiery emerald gaze, and witnessing his cocksure grin, her heart gave a tiny flip-flop of realization. It was useless to deny that what had transpired between them was anything less than powerful, and nothing even remotely close to resembling friendship.

And that meant trouble for her. Big trouble.

8

HE'D PLAYED DIRTY. Austin had acknowledged that fact minutes after Teddy left his house Monday evening, but three days later, he still didn't regret his unabashed behavior in prodding her to admit there was something between them. Her admission hadn't been verbal, but that mind-blowing kiss she'd initiated spoke volumes.

At first, he'd been annoyed that she'd had the nerve to ask him for yet another favor, but during the course of their conversation, he'd seen glimpses of contradicting emotions, of her wanting him as much as he wanted her, and a latent fear that kept her from completely opening herself to him. It had been that honest vulnerability that had softened him. Though he'd accepted her invitation for Christmas Eve, he'd been the one to establish the rules. No pretenses. So far, she'd adhered to his personal request, accepting and openly responding to the intimate kiss he'd greeted her with when he'd arrived at her condo to pick her up.

The woman was an inherently sensual creature, and despite her reservations, she certainly indulged wholeheartedly in kissing him, and took pleasure in the way he touched her. The low-cut, clingy red knit dress she'd worn in celebration of Christmas had tempted his hands to skim those ultrafeminine curves of hers—from the sleek line of her spine, over her bottom, and up and around to her hips, her waist, to just below the gentle slope of her breasts where his thumbs brushed along those full, soft mounds.

She'd moaned in acquiescence and arched toward him for a deeper, more provocative contact, but he'd resisted the invitation. Satisfying the hunger he'd tasted in her kiss would take more than the few minutes they had before leaving for her parents'. The woman was in need of personal attention, emotionally and physically, and he planned to give her as much as she could handle, and then some, until she came to the realization that what was between them was worth pursuing.

Satisfied with his plan, Austin glanced over at Teddy sitting in the passenger seat of the Mustang as they drove to her parents' house in Pacific Heights. She was rummaging through her purse for something, and he switched on the overhead reading light for her. She smiled her thanks and withdrew a tube of lipstick.

"So, how are things with Louden?" he asked, curious if his presence at the company Christmas party had made any difference in her boss's attitude.

Flipping down the lighted mirror in front of her, she uncapped the tube and covered her kiss-swollen lips with a slash of pink-cinnamon color. "Just fine," she said too brightly.

He frowned as he made a left-hand turn onto the street Teddy had indicated. "Is he leaving you alone?"

She fluffed her hair that he'd unintentionally mussed during their kiss. She had the silkiest hair, and he loved running his fingers though the warm strands. She didn't seem to mind his fascination with her hair, either.

"I'm beginning to realize that Louden has the morals of an alley cat," she said, her tone tempered with disgust. "Which means he'll continue to prey until a bigger cat comes along and knocks him down a peg or two."

A flare of possessiveness gripped him, and his hands tightened on the steering wheel. "How about I pay Louden a personal visit and let him know just how close he is to being neutered?"

She laughed, but the sound was strained. "Austin, I can handle Louden. By the end of the next week, one way or another, this will all be over with. I'll either get the promotion, or I won't."

She didn't sound very positive, and that bothered him. "And if you don't?"

"Then I update my résumé and start over," she said in quiet resignation, putting the lighted mirror back in its place. "And I can't begin to tell you how much I dread doing that. It means proving myself all over again."

He heard the frustration in her voice, and knew she was referring to more than just establishing herself with another employer, but with her family, too. Strangely enough, he understood her resentment, and respected her determination to overcome it.

Reaching across the console, he gently laid his hand on her knee, offering silent support. "Getting that promotion is really important to you, isn't it?"

"Yeah, it is, for so many reasons," she admitted, then drew a deep breath as if to dismiss the entire subject. "Turn right here, then make another right on Vallejo. My parents' house is on the left-hand side."

He followed Teddy's directions, impressed with the ritzy area of San Francisco and multimillion-dollar homes overlooking the Bay, even though he'd expected as much. Trying not to allow old insecurities to assail him, he made the final turn onto Vallejo Street, determined to make the best impression on Teddy's family that he could, and hoped they accepted him for who he was. Nothing more. Nothing less.

"Which house?" he asked, glancing at Teddy. He frowned when he saw her struggling with the ruby and diamond band she wore on her ring finger.

"Stop the car for a minute," she said, her tone exasperated.

He slowed the Mustang to a halt as close to the side of the narrow road as he could, put the vehicle in park, and turned to face her. "What are you doing?"

She tugged and twisted on the band, her face contorted with frustration. "I'm trying to take off my ring."

"Why?"

She exhaled loudly and continued her determined attempt to remove the ring, which refused to slip over her first knuckle. "Because my parents gave me this band when I graduated from high school, and they've never seen it on my left hand."

He couldn't help the grin spreading across his face. "Ah, so the illusion of being 'taken' is for every one else's benefit, but not your family's."

"Yeah, something like that," she muttered vaguely.

He continued to watch her struggle, amused with her thinking. "Don't you think you're making the issue more complicated than it needs to be?"

"No." Her succinct answer segued into a wince of pain, then a very unladylike curse when the gold cut into her flesh. "I must be retaining water," she said hopelessly.

Taking pity on her, he reached for her left hand. "Here, let me help."

"What?" she asked incredulously as he examined her finger. "You've got a pair of clippers in your glove box to cut the ring off my finger?"

He chuckled at her sarcasm. "Nope. Don't need any."

She snorted in disbelief. "Well, that ring isn't going to come off any other way..."

Her sassy comment rolled into a surprised gasp as he lifted her palm and used his tongue to dampen the skin where the ring encircled the digit, then closed his mouth over her finger to moisten the entire length. He suckled gently, swirling his tongue up and down her finger, thoroughly wetting her sensitized skin. Her eyes widened, her hand went limp in his, and an arousing groan slipped past her parted lips.

Once he was confident that her skin was slick enough, he dragged her finger from his mouth and gave the ring a twist and a gentle tug. The band slipped to her knuckle, and tightened around the bone. She let out a discouraged sigh, but he wasn't about to admit defeat, and slipped her finger into his mouth again, using his teeth and tongue to work the ring over her knuckle.

This time, he succeeded. Removing the band from his mouth, he turned her hand over and dropped the ring onto her palm.

"Thank you," she said breathlessly.

"Anytime." He grinned wickedly. "Do you need help putting it on your other finger?"

She quickly shook her head, but not before he saw the spark of desire that colored her brown eyes. "I think I can manage on my own." She did the deed herself, without any problems.

Putting the car into drive, he eased back into the street. "If you insist on wearing a ring on your left-hand finger, you need to think about getting yourself one that fits." He extended the comment mildly, but a fleeting, possessive thought crossed his mind as he turned into the Spencers' driveway. He wanted to be the one to put a ring there.

"So, Austin, how did you and my daughter meet?" The elder Evan Spencer the third asked as he handed Austin the double shot of Bailey's he'd poured for him.

Austin glanced around the expensively furnished parlor, complete with a professionally decorated twelve-foot blue spruce, and noted that all eyes were on him—from Teddy's parents, to each one of her three brothers and their respective wives, to Teddy herself. The eight nieces and nephews he'd met in a blur upon arriving were now in an adjoining playroom, watching videos, playing on the pinball and arcade games, and from the sounds of their laughter, having a good time with all the high-tech toys Grandma and Grandpa had purchased for their enjoyment.

"Yes, *how* did you meet?" Teddy's mother, Gloria, insisted on knowing. She tilted her blond head questioningly, appearing very much the well-bred hostess.

Teddy stood a few feet away, next to her mother, her luminous gaze pleading with him to be gentle with his answer.

No pretenses, he'd told her, yet he found he didn't want to embarrass Teddy, either. He'd only known the Spencers for less than half an hour, yet he got the distinct impression that Teddy's parents would find the truth distasteful and him unsuitable for their only daughter. The last thing he wanted was two strikes against him before he had a chance to convince Teddy how good they could be together.

He grinned at everyone, then settled his gaze on Teddy, giving her a private smile. "We met on her birthday, at the Frisco Bay."

Gratitude colored Teddy's eyes, but her relief was short-lived.

Gloria gasped, her hand fluttering to the pearl necklace layering the front of her cream silk blouse as she stared at her daughter in mortification. "You were picked up in a bar?"

Susan and Natalie, two of Teddy's sisters-in-law who were sitting next to each other on the sofa, smothered amused laughter. The sympathetic look they sent Austin's way led him to believe that their mother-in-law's theatrical display was a normal occurrence.

"No, Mother," Teddy said patiently. "I was with Brenda and Laura, having a drink for my birthday, and Austin didn't 'pick me up.' He was very much a gentleman, and we hit it off well."

"So well that she took him to her Christmas party," Susan announced, just in case that tidbit of information hadn't made the rounds.

"Wow, must be serious, Theodora," Teddy's oldest brother, Evan, Jr., commented, winking at his little sister. "It's been so long since you've dated, we were beginning to worry that you were thinking about joining a convent."

Teddy glared at her brother. "You live to torment me, Evan."

"You're wrong, Evan," her other brother, Russ, added. "She'd rather be a CEO than a nun."

That earned a harrumph from her father. "I just don't understand you and your silly whims, Teddy," Evan, Sr., said sternly, swirling his martini. "We raised you to be a respectable young woman—"

"I'm an *independent* woman," Teddy interrupted her father's tirade.

"No argument there," Brent agreed with a grin. "Independent, stubborn and full of sass." Brent saluted Austin with his own drink of Jack Daniel's and soda. "If you can handle the independent gal, you can have her."

"No man worth his salt is going to allow his wife to work," the senior Evans said gruffly. Susan rolled her eyes as if to state she'd heard this lecture before, and the other two merely shook their heads.

"Isn't that right, Austin?" Evan, Sr., asked, looking for approval.

The cable-knit sweater Austin had worn suddenly felt heavy, hot and suffocating. Teddy's three sisters-in-law leaned forward in their seats, looking on in avid interest. Her brothers were obviously finding a lot of humor in the situation, and Teddy's mother was standing by her man and his old-fashioned ways. Even Teddy's expression showed she was curious about his answer.

This one he had to ride out on his own, and since there was only one person he wanted to please, he spoke the truth. "Well, sir, I'm all for a woman working and having a career, if that's what she really wants."

The three sisters-in-law grinned at one another, as if Austin's statement had marked a major milestone in the Spencer household. Something in Teddy's gaze softened perceptibly, and Austin grasped and held on to the emotion, tucking it away for later.

"And who'll stay home and raise the kids?" Evan, Sr., argued.

"Dad, this is a moot point," Teddy interrupted before Austin could reply, her cheeks flushed a faint shade of pink. "I have no intention of getting married anytime soon, let alone having kids."

Her father shook a finger at her. "You're too stubborn for your own good, Theodora."

Russ stepped up to his father and slapped him good-naturedly on the back. "Dad, I think she's got you beat on this one."

"She already passed up one great catch," Gloria interjected. "How many others will she go through before she runs out of suitable men to marry?"

Evan, Sr., glanced at his only daughter, frowning. "I don't know many men who'll wait around while a woman chases after a fanciful hobby that keeps her too occupied to be a proper wife."

The hurt in Teddy's eyes was unmistakable, as was the resignation that her parents would never understand her choices.

The maid announced dinner, dispelling the awkward moment, and the family moved to the formal dining room. Austin remained behind with Teddy for a few extra seconds while she regained her composure.

"It's like this every time," Teddy said wearily.

Not knowing what to say to that, Austin touched his hand to the small of her back in a supportive gesture as they entered the adjoining room. Her parents didn't understand what drove Teddy, but he certainly did. The woman was strong and independent, but what no one realized was just how much her struggle to establish her own individuality was costing her emotionally.

Beneath a glittering chandelier, a long cherry-wood table was draped with cream linen and set with fine china, gleaming silver and elegant crystal. The adults sat at the formal table, while the kids were served at the picnic-style table in the game room established just for them.

The meal was an enjoyable feast of rack of lamb, sweet potatoes, fresh green beans and warm, crusty bread. Dinner conversation centered around Teddy's brother's professions of surgeon, lawyer and optometrist, and the various charities her mother and sisters-in-law had donated their time to during the holidays. All in all, Austin found the discussions entertaining, shared his opinion when asked, and enjoyed the humor and anecdotes thrown in by Teddy's brothers and sisters-in-law. It had been a long time since he'd been in a family setting, and it reminded him just how lonely his own life was when Jordan wasn't around.

They made it all the way to coffee and a rich, decadent dessert of chocolate truffle cheesecake without incident, when Evan, Sr., leaned back in his chair at the head of the table and addressed Austin specifically.

"So, Austin, what are your intentions toward Teddy?" The question was asked congenially enough, but Austin didn't doubt the seriousness behind the query.

Teddy stiffened beside him. "Dad!" she whispered harshly, obviously mortified.

Gloria, who sat on the other side of Teddy, patted her daughter's hand consolingly. "Now, Theodora, your father is just looking out for your welfare."

Austin smothered a grin as he watched that chin of Teddy's lift mutinously and fire enter her eyes. "I'm a big girl, Mother, and more than capable of taking care of myself."

"Well?" the senior Evans prompted, ignoring Teddy's statement.

Austin did a quick survey of the other residents at the table, none of whom looked ready to jump to his defense. "Intentions?" He mulled over the word while taking a drink of his coffee. "Well, I hadn't really thought of Teddy in those terms. I care for your daughter very much. I guess we'll have to see where it leads."

Evan, Sr., nodded and rubbed his chin thoughtfully. "Can you support her appropriately?"

Teddy nearly choked on the bite of cheesecake she'd been swallowing. Once her coughing fit was under control, she cast a beseeching glance her father's way. "*Dad,*" she said between gritted teeth, the word sounding suspiciously like a warning.

"Now, Theodora," her mother chastised. "These are

perfectly legitimate questions for your father to ask of any young man who expresses an interest in you."

"Or a *woman* who might express an interest in one of your brothers," Susan added oh-so-helpfully, letting Austin know that no one was safe from the elder Spencers' interrogation.

"I'm not rich by any stretch of the imagination," Austin admitted, pushing aside his half-eaten dessert. "But the house I live in is paid for, and I make a decent living, certainly enough to support a family."

An inquisitive look entered Evan, Sr.'s, gaze. "I don't believe you've said what you do for a living."

"He's an investment broker," Teddy announced eagerly, the same moment that Austin said, "I own my own landscaping business."

It didn't take a rocket scientist to guess that Teddy had feared he'd reveal his Fantasy for Hire gig.

Dead silence followed, and everybody seemed to go perfectly still as eight pair of eyes scrutinized him like an insect under a microscope. Even Teddy seemed to stop breathing, and he couldn't help wondering if she'd approve of what he *really* did for a living—digging ditches.

"You're a busy man, Mr. McBride," Brent said with some degree of amusement, breaking up the stagnant silence that had settled in the dining room.

"Certainly very enterprising," Evan, Sr., agreed, sounding begrudgingly impressed.

"Actually, I'm no longer an investment broker," he said, certain he saw Teddy's shoulders slump at that announcement. "I'm concentrating on the landscaping business."

"Oh," Gloria said, and the sound wasn't a complimentary one.

Austin knew if he intended to see Teddy again, he

wanted the truth out on the table now. "I know landscaping doesn't sound as glamorous as an investment broker. It's a lot of hard work, and some days long hours, but overall I find it very satisfying."

Evan, Sr., glanced from Teddy, then back to the man she'd brought to meet their family. Austin was certain he wasn't what the elder Spencer and his wife had in mind for their daughter, but Austin was exactly what he said he was. What they saw was what they got.

"And your parents," Evan, Sr., went on, as if striving to find some redeeming quality. "What do they do?"

"Both of my parents are dead." Knowing he had nothing left to lose, he added, "It's just me and my brother, Jordan, who is currently an unemployed architect."

Dismay filled Gloria's eyes as she looked at Teddy, as if she couldn't believe her daughter had settled for less than one of the prominent businessmen in their league.

Teddy's five-year-old niece, Katie, came out of the playroom at that moment, anticipation wreathing her pretty face. "Grandma, we all ate our dinner. When do we get to open our presents?"

An adoring smile softened Gloria's features as she looked at her granddaughter, and Austin had the thought that this woman was a marshmallow beneath her haughty exterior. "I suppose now would be a good time, since you all have to get to bed soon so Santa can come visit. Why don't you get everyone to wash up and meet us in the parlor?"

Katie raced from the room, her little-girl voice announcing to her cousins, "We get to open our presents!"

The adults laughed at the responding squeals of delight and "yipees" that drifted from the playroom, and they all moved back into the parlor. Austin made himself comfortable on the sofa while Teddy helped pass out the gaily wrapped Christmas presents under the tree, obviously having fun with the task. For as much as she'd claimed that kids weren't her forte, Austin couldn't help noticing how much she enjoyed playing the role of aunt, and how loving she was with each child. A smile played at the corner of his mouth as he watched Teddy divide her attention between helping Drew, her three-year-old nephew, put together a chunky wooden puzzle, and her six-year-old niece, Molly, diaper her new "Baby-wets-a-lot." Her maternal instincts weren't as suppressed as she might want to believe.

Susan settled herself next to Austin, and he smiled amicably at her. There was mischief in the other woman's gaze, and a glint of determination. Leaning close, taking advantage of Gloria and Evan, Sr.'s, distraction, she said in a low voice, "Don't sweat the small stuff, Austin. The Spencers are a different breed. Everyone goes through the initial interrogation process. What ultimately matters is how Teddy feels about you."

Austin appreciated Susan's encouragement, but after that enlightening dinner conversation, he wasn't so sure fitting into Teddy's life would be as easy as surviving the Spencer's third-degree. Not only did he feel as though he'd never measure up, he honestly had no idea where he stood with Teddy—if what he did for a living mattered to her, or how she truly felt about him—beyond their "agreements."

Maybe it was time he found out.

9

TEDDY LEANED her head against the passenger seat's headrest and released a long pent-up breath—in relief, exhaustion and a good part frustration. Beside her, Austin was quiet as he pulled out of her parents' driveway, the moonlight reflected through the windshield illuminating his pensive features.

"That was a disaster," she said, shaking her head in disappointment.

"Not the entire evening," he graciously conceded with a smile that wasn't quite as sexy and breathtaking as usual. "I enjoyed watching the kids open their presents, and talking to your brothers and their wives."

Her siblings seemed to like him, too, which pleased her. However, Teddy didn't miss the fact that he had no compliments for her parents—not that they'd deserved any accolades after the way they'd grilled him. "I never would have thought my parents would behave so atrociously," she said, her tone contrite.

He brought the car to a halt at a stop sign and glanced over at her, his gaze expressing an odd combination of understanding and regret. Reaching across the console, he gently brushed his fingers along her cheek. "I suppose they're just concerned about who their little girl is getting involved with."

Her skin tingled where he touched her, eliciting a sensual warmth that spread through her entire body. "As if they have any say in the matter," she said, forcing an indignant note over the quiver of awareness infusing her voice. "If my parents had their choice, they'd have me married off to some stuffy blue blood, being a *proper* wife."

"I can't imagine it," he murmured, a sly smile curving his mouth.

She exaggerated a shudder, adding to the humor of the situation. "Neither can I."

They both laughed, his low, husky chuckles mingling with her lighter ones, the sound pleasant and very intimate in the close confines of the car. The lighthearted moment released some of the tension she'd sensed in him a half hour after arriving at her parents'. The evening had only gotten worse, and certainly more complicated than she'd expected.

Austin drove on, maneuvering the car through the streets of Pacific Heights. He wasn't taking the normal way back to her condo, but she didn't mind if he wanted to take a longer route, which would give her more time with him. It was Christmas Eve, and for the first time since she could remember, she dreaded being alone.

"Austin..." She fiddled with the strap of her purse. "I'm really sorry for my parents' behavior tonight, and that you had to lie about owning your own landscaping business. I'll be the first to admit that my parents can be judgmental, but they'll come around."

He glanced her way. "You planning on bringing me to another family get-together?"

Her heart thumped in her chest, and a flood of emotions shook her to her soul. There was no denying she enjoyed everything about Austin, from his humor and honesty, to the feminine way he made her feel. But he made her yearn for things that conflicted with everything she'd worked so hard to attain, and the strength of those feelings frightened her.

She gave a noncommittal shrug, which was the best she could offer him. "You never know."

He stared at her for a long, intense moment, then switched his gaze back to the road. "Does it matter to you what I do for a living?" he asked quietly.

She glanced out her window to the darkness beyond, giving his question serious consideration. If she was honest with herself, she had to admit that on some level Austin owning Fantasy for Hire bothered her, because she disliked the thought that other women fantasized about him and lusted over that gorgeous body while he performed a sexy striptease for them. She was beginning to think of Austin as *her* fantasy, and she didn't want to share. Jealousy was a foreign emotion to her, one she'd never experienced in a relationship with a man, but she quickly realized she wasn't immune to the green-eyed monster.

So how did she answer his question without sounding like a possessive shrew? "I'd be lying if I said it didn't matter to me what you did for a living. But I suppose I can learn to get used to you stripping for other women."

"And what if I really did own my own landscaping business?" he asked, his voice slightly anxious. "Would that line of work make a difference to you?"

She studied his face, seeing the taut line of his jaw, the tense set of his shoulders beneath his cable-knit sweater, and the truth finally dawned on her. "You really are in that line of work, aren't you? Along with Fantasy for Hire."

He nodded, and turned onto another darkened street that climbed upward and overlooked Pacific Heights. "Yep. McBride Commercial Landscaping is a real, solid business. I'm not rich, but I'm successful enough to support myself, and I love my job."

She tilted her head, fascinated with this facet of Austin's life. "And Fantasy for Hire?"

"It's been a lucrative business, and it helped to support me when I needed the money, but I've definitely outgrown it. I'm going to sell the business so I can devote my time to McBride Landscaping."

The car rolled to a stop. Austin cut the engine and turned to look at her with searching eyes, as if gauging her reaction to his newest revelation. It struck her then, that as confident as Austin appeared, he harbored a few insecurities of his own.

"Why does what I think matter so much to you?" she whispered, breaking through the quiet that had settled in the car.

"Because this is who I am, Teddy," he said, his warm gaze falling from her eyes, to her mouth, then back up again. "What you see is what you get, and I want to be sure you're okay with that."

Liquid heat pooled in her belly. "Yeah, I am."

"I'm not some blue blood with a fancy investment-broker image, Teddy—"

She pressed her fingers to his lips to stop his words, and the jolt of electrical heat that passed between them made her shiver. "That's probably why I'm so attracted to you."

Gently, he grasped her wrist, lowering her hand so her palm pressed against his chest, so she could feel the steady beating of his heart. "And your parents?"

She understood the reassurances he was searching for. Her mother and father hadn't issued full approval of Austin, and he wanted to make sure it made no difference to her. "Do you honestly think it matters to me what my parents think?"

His eyes burned into hers, hot and filled with an honest, primitive need that tapped into every responding nerve in her body. "I just want to be sure before we go any further."

Knowing where the next step in their relationship would lead, an equal measure of excitement and apprehension swirled within her. "I'm...sure."

The lazy, sexy grin that settled on his mouth was sheer male, and the dark look in his green eyes was very, very pleased.

Needing a moment to absorb what she'd just agreed to, she glanced around at their surroundings. Wherever he'd parked was pitch-black and deserted. They were alone, except for the breathless view of the bay below them and the star-studded sky above. A renewed rush of warmth seeped into her midsection.

"Where are we?" she asked, peering out the window.

His long fingers trailed along her shoulder and toyed with her silky hair. "It's a secluded place that not many people know about."

She cast him a teasing look. "And how do you know about it?"

He grinned, a wicked light brightening his gaze. "When I was in high school, I'd bring girls up here to make out with them." He looked off in the distance, amusement in his expression. "One time, when I was sixteen and had just gotten my driver's license, I brought a girl up here on a Saturday night. Not fifteen minutes later, another car pulled up, and it was Jordan and his date." Austin chuckled, shaking his head. "He didn't so much as get the chance to kiss his girl, because he was so furious at finding me up here, making out with my date."

Teddy laughed at the fond memory he shared, reminded too much of how her own brothers had been with the guys she'd dated. Protective and ruthless. "It must be an older-brother thing."

His thumb rubbed along her sensitive earlobe, then found the spot that made her shiver with pleasure. "You got caught necking, too?"

"No, never. I missed out on that particular fun." She sighed with a small measure of regret, because she'd been too busy with debutante balls and country-club dances. And though she'd been rebellious enough to go along with the suggestion, no boy had issued the invitation. "I just meant that my brothers were overly protective of me, too. Who I went out with, where my dates took me, and all that stuff. Not that they had anything to worry about. The boys I was allowed to date came from prestigious families that were friends of my parents, and they wouldn't have dared touched me the wrong way. I was deemed a 'good girl,' and my brothers made sure I kept that reputation."

"Well, you're all grown up, your brothers aren't anywhere around, and I'm not one of those saps who come from a highfalutin family." He leaned close, and her senses spun at the hot, hungry look in his eyes. "Wanna neck?"

Being a bad girl suddenly held enormous appeal. Feeling reckless, she met him halfway to the console. "Yeah, I think I do."

The hand caressing her throat moved up and slid into her hair, threading through the warm strands. The last thing she saw was the sinful grin curving his mouth, then his lips covered hers and he was kissing her—long, deeply intimate kisses that brought her to a fever pitch of need in no time flat. Her body swelled with arousal, her breasts grew heavy, and an achy emptiness settled in the pit of her belly.

They made out like two lust-filled teenagers, both attempting to find a comfortable position that would allow them more freedom to use their hands without putting a crick in their necks. Austin managed to cup her breast in his hand, and when she shifted to move closer, his arm twisted awkwardly and fell away. She touched his thigh, but the other hand supporting her slipped off the console and she nearly bit his lip as the impact jarred her entire body.

A giggle escaped her. "This is crazy."

He nuzzled her neck, his breath hot and damp against her skin. "But fun and kinda sexy, don't you think?"

Delicious and thrilling, she agreed, if only her back didn't ache from her awkward position. "I can't get close enough," she complained.

"Yeah, you can." Moving back to his side of the car, he slid the leather seat back, making more room between him and the steering wheel. "C'mere, Teddy," he murmured huskily, his eyes ablaze with a sweet, sexual promise that dared her to be just as bold. "I want you to sit on my lap so I can touch you the way I've been wanting to since the night of the Christmas party."

His words made her shiver, made her melt, made her eager for what they both wanted. Judging the distance between them and deeming it as too far, she climbed over the console with his help, but not without whacking her leg on the steering wheel, losing a shoe on the trek and elbowing him in the ribs. They laughed at their bumbling, but all amusement ceased once she was straddling his thighs...their embrace so snug and intimate there was no mistaking how much he wanted her.

He skimmed her hips with his hands and smiled a roguish grin that told her he'd had way too much experience as a young teen at this sort of thing. "Close enough for you?"

"Yeah." Her fingers found their way beneath the hem of his sweater. His flat abdomen clenched as she stroked his belly, luxuriating in his vibrant, muscular body. "Can I take off your sweater?"

"Honey, you can do anything to me that you'd like to," he urged. "Be as bad as you want to be. I won't tell a soul."

Licking her dry lips, and enjoying the thrill of being naughty, she lifted the cable-knit over his head and spent a minute exploring his magnificent chest and the hot, tight feel of his skin all the way down to the waistband of his slacks. His hips rolled enthusiastically beneath her, but instead of giving him the attention he sought, she touched her knees, which bracketed his hips. Slowly, she skimmed her palms upward, dragging the hem of her knit dress up her thighs, tempting him with the lacy band holding up her silk stockings and a glimpse of smooth, pale skin.

His breathing deepened as he watched her brazen, shameless display on his lap, and she gently tipped his chin up with a finger so his eyes met hers. Not quite done seducing him, she grasped one of the hands cinching her waist and flattened his palm at the base of her throat, then guided his hot, callused fingers inside the low-cut collar of her dress.

Stopping just above where the upper slope of her breast swelled from her bra, she whispered invitingly in the shadowed interior of the vehicle, "Touch me the way you've been wanting to since the Christmas party."

With a low-throated growl, he slipped the shoulders of her dress down, until the stretchy material tightened around her arms, and the front bunched around her waist. He didn't bother with the back clasp to her sheer, lacy bra, and instead lowered the cups so that her breasts sprang free from the binding—firm, full and eager for attention. His hands shaped her, his thumbs rasped across her sensitive nipples, and then he dipped his head and took one puckered tip into his hot, wet mouth.

Moaning in pure, unadulterated pleasure, Teddy let her head drop back, arched her spine and clenched her fingers in his thick, soft hair. He teased the crest with his teeth, then soothed the gentle bites with the damp swirl of his tongue until her breasts grew swollen and heavy.

Her flesh thrummed. Her blood pounded. A sultry heat swirled within the car, making her skin slick, and his just as damp. Idly, she noticed that the windows were completely fogged, cocooning them in their own private world. The arousing, male scent of him filled every panting breath she gulped, and suddenly she wasn't near close enough for what she needed. Gripping his bare shoulders, she rocked into him, so that the hard ridge beneath the fly of his pants pressed against the apex of her thighs, rubbing enticingly. She gasped at the erotic friction of wet silk against pulsing, aroused flesh. He groaned and grew impossibly thicker.

A ragged sob caught in her throat, and she grappled frantically with the thin leather belt at his waist, wanting to touch him, stroke him, feel him inside her where she needed him the most.

He caught her wrists, laughing harshly, stopping her before she attained her goal. She gazed down at him in confusion, finding nothing humorous about the situation.

His smoky gaze flickered over her, taking in her wanton display on his lap—the way the front of her dress was pulled low to reveal the pale curves of her breasts, and the hem that flashed a tempting expanse of thigh and held the promise of something far more alluring. She trembled, as if he'd physically stroked her in all those inflamed places.

Visibly drawing in a steady breath, he brought his gaze back to hers. "Teddy, honey, I want you so badly I can't think straight. But I don't have any protection with me, and I won't risk you that way."

She closed her eyes, ignoring the deep, internal throb demanding release, but her attempts failed. "You're experienced at this sort of thing," she said, frowning playfully at him. "Didn't you come prepared?"

A rakish grin slashed across his features at her complaint. "Not to make love to you. When we do, I want a nice, soft bed beneath us, and hours to enjoy us being together, not a quickie in my car."

She rolled her eyes in mock disgust. "What a time to be chivalrous."

A deep chuckle rumbled in his chest. Letting go of her hands, he nuzzled her neck, skimming his lips up to her ear. "You'll thank me later, but right now, let me take the edge off for you."

She opened her mouth to tell him no, that she didn't want to experience that sexual release without him, but those clever hands of his were already rasping along her stockings and disappearing beneath the hem of her dress. He stroked the soft, sensitive flesh of her inner thighs, and the only sound that emerged from between her lips was a low, needy groan.

Her hips shifted, tilting toward him instinctively. His fingers leisurely traced the elastic band of her panties along the crease of her leg, brushed erotically over the strip of silk covering her feminine secrets, then finally slipped beneath that barrier to glide his thumb over that slick, aching bud of flesh.

A shock wave of pleasure rolled through her. She bit

her bottom lip to keep from crying out and squeezed her eyes shut to maintain some control. He made her wild. He made her shameless. Her body never felt so vibrantly alive, and the foreign sensation was as thrilling as it was startling.

"Look at me, Teddy." Austin's voice was dark and coaxing, gentle and reassuring.

She tried. Oh, Lord, she tried—barely managing to lift her lashes and meet his dark, hungry gaze. He sat back in his seat, watching her, his muscular body tense, his breathing just as erratic as hers as his fingers continued to ply a delicious, forbidden kind of magic.

She quivered from head to toe, and pressed her hands against his chest for support. Uncertainties assailed her. "Austin..."

"Shh..." Somehow, someway, he understood her fears of letting go. "I want to watch you, just like this." He stroked her slowly, rhythmically, building the exquisite pressure. "You're incredibly beautiful, Teddy, and very sexy...come for me."

His words, his touch, the reverent way he looked at her, pushed her to the edge, then over that precipice. While he watched, she came undone for him, letting the climax roll over her in waves of intense pleasure that seemed to go on and on. A long, low moan ripped from her, and he groaned right along with her, the provocative sound setting off additional surges of sensation that extended the deep, internal shudders rippling through her body.

Satiated, she collapsed against his chest, burying her face in the crook of his neck as she struggled to breathe normally. The interior of the car was warm and humid from the heat they'd generated, and her breasts slid against his damp chest, arousing her all over again.

Austin adjusted the top of her dress, covering her, then

smoothed his hands down her spine in a languid caress. "You're incredible, Teddy."

Smiling drowsily, she lifted her head and brushed her fingers across his lips, reveling in the contentment she felt with this man. "I think you deserve all the credit for what just happened."

His grin was pure male satisfaction, and she discovered that she didn't want this night to end. Not this soon.

"Austin, I know it's Christmas Eve, and you probably spend Christmas morning with Jordan, but I don't want to be alone tonight." She swallowed hard. The admission cost her emotionally, but her need for him went beyond anything she'd ever experienced. "If you have a few spare condoms we can use, I have a nice, soft bed at home we can make good use of." Her tone was light and teasing, but her insides tied up in knots at the thought that he might refuse her.

He smoothed her disheveled hair from her face. The undeniable need reflecting in his eyes eased her fears of rejection. The rakish grin tipping the corners of his mouth made her heart swell with powerful emotions. "The condoms are at home."

She worried her bottom lip between her teeth, briefly considering her brazen request. "Maybe you could drop me off at my place, then go and get them, and a spare change of clothes?"

He stared at her, searching her expression—for what, she couldn't be certain. "Are you sure about this, Teddy?"

For a moment, her heart faltered. Trapped by the hunger glittering in his eyes, her breath fluttered in her throat. He wasn't asking for a lifetime commitment, she told herself, just the certainty that she was ready for a more intimate relationship. Adults indulged in mutual pleasure all the time, and she desperately craved that sensual connection with him.

"Yeah, I'm sure," she whispered. Framing his face between her hands, she lowered her parted lips to his to prove just how certain she was about becoming his lover.

A rapid tapping against Austin's window startled Teddy, and it took a few heartbeats and Austin's comical expression for her to realize that someone had caught them making out. Horrified at the prospect, but grateful for the fogged windows which offered a modicum of privacy, she scrambled back to her side of the car. Her dress caught on the gearshift, and the vehicle rocked with her swift movement over the console. Finding Austin's sweater on the floorboard, she tossed it at him.

"Put that on!" she ordered frantically.

"Kinda late for modesty, don't you think?" he drawled, tugging the sweater over his head and adjusting it over his torso.

She glared at him, tamping down the bubble of laughter working its way up. The situation was hilarious, if not a bit humiliating, but she wasn't going to give him the satisfaction of humoring him.

"Hey, kids, roll down the window," a gruff voice commanded. "It's past curfew, and I don't think your parents would appreciate being called down to the police station on Christmas Eve."

Austin did as he was instructed, rolling his window halfway down while Teddy gave the hem of her dress a fierce tug, stretching the material to her knees. "Good evening, sir," he said respectfully to the uniformed officer standing outside the Mustang.

The cop crouched down, and a beam of light searched the interior of the car, bouncing from Austin to Teddy. Her cheeks flamed with embarrassment.

The officer grinned, clearly expecting teenagers, not two grown adults. "Considering you're both consenting adults, I'm guessing your parents wouldn't give a damn if you spent the night in the slammer."

"Uh, no, sir," Austin replied politely.

The cop snapped off his light. "I'll give you five minutes for the windows to clear, then I suggest you take this to a private place," he said, amusement obvious in his voice.

Austin nodded his gratitude. "We'll do that, sir."

The officer headed back to his squad car, and Austin turned and grinned impishly at her. "Well, you've just experienced the full effect of making out on a dark, secluded road." He turned the ignition and put the window defroster on full blast. "That was probably just as embarrassing as getting caught by one of your brothers."

Teddy groaned and slumped against her seat. "Thank you for the unique experience."

Austin winked at her. "It was my pleasure."

AUSTIN STUFFED a clean change of clothes into his duffel bag, then crossed the wooden floor of his room to the bathroom, the spurs he'd attached to his cowboy boots jangling with each impatient step. Grabbing his toothbrush and a few other necessities, he returned to the bed, tossed the toiletries into the duffel, then went to retrieve the most important item for his sleep-over at Teddy's.

Just as he withdrew the unopened box of condoms he'd had stashed in his nightstand for the past six months, he heard a brisk knock on the open bedroom door. Like a kid being caught with something forbidden, the tips of his ears warmed, and he discreetly buried the box in his bag. His reaction was insane, considering he was a grown man, but there was something about Teddy that made what was going to happen tonight special. He didn't want to spoil his own mood, or tarnish Teddy's reputation, by enduring Jordan's ribbing.

However, explaining the costume he was wearing was something he hadn't considered.

Reluctantly, he turned to face Jordan, who was leaning against the doorjamb, his hands buried in the pockets of his robe.

A grin twitched the corners of Jordan's mouth as he took in Austin's cowboy attire, complete with Stetson, chaps and shiny silver spurs he'd bought to complete the Fantasy for Hire ensemble.

Jordan moved into the bedroom, curiosity brimming in his eyes. "I was expecting to hear Santa tonight, but the jangling noise I heard didn't sound like Christmas bells, so I thought I'd better investigate."

Austin zipped up the duffel, anxious to be on his way. "I'm sorry if I woke you up."

"Where in the world are you going dressed like that on Christmas Eve?" Jordan's amusement faded into a frown of disapproval. "Don't tell me that you've got a gig tonight."

Austin was beginning to feel like tonight's "gig" would be the performance of his life. Slinging the duffel over his shoulder, he grinned at his brother. "Don't wait up for me, pardner," he drawled humorously, tipping his Stetson at Jordan. "I've got one last fantasy to fulfill, and I have a feeling it's going to take all night long."

A slow grin spread across Jordan's face as understanding dawned.

Before Jordan could comment, Austin headed out the door and down the stairs. The metallic sound of the spurs' rowels chinking against wood rang throughout the house.

Jordan stood at the top of the stairs, and called after

Austin, "Be careful that you don't hurt Teddy with those spurs!"

Austin chuckled. It was obvious that his brother adored Teddy as much as he did. Now it was just a matter of convincing Teddy how much she belonged in his life.

10

Austin didn't know what to expect when he returned to Teddy's condo, but it certainly wasn't the sultry vixen who greeted him. Just like him, Teddy had changed, but her attire was far more enticing, and certainly more revealing. Soft chiffon and sheer lace in a deep shade of purple shaped her full breasts and draped along her curves to midthigh, accentuating everything womanly about her. Her hair was tousled around her head, her eyes shone bright with anticipation, and she smelled delicious, like citrus and something infinitely soft and feminine.

"Very nice," he murmured appreciatively, forgetting all about the role he'd wanted to play for her.

She shifted anxiously on her feet, and the hem of the nightie flirted along her thighs. "I got the nightgown for my birthday, and I thought I'd put it to good use," she explained, a faint blush touching her cheeks.

He didn't bother to point out that she wouldn't be wearing it for long.

He waited for her to invite him in, but she didn't seem in any hurry to do so. Her gaze leisurely traveled the length of him, and he could have sworn he heard her breath catch when she reached the spurs attached to his boots. There was no mistaking the excitement wreathing her expression when she glanced back at his face.

"Hello, cowboy," she said in a husky, come-hither voice.

He touched the brim of his hat politely, ignoring the swift current of heat rushing through his veins so he could play along with the fantasy he wanted to create for her. "Ma'am."

Her small, pink tongue licked her bottom lip, and she leaned against the wall in the entryway, looking entirely too tempting. Blinking innocently, she asked, "So, cowboy, what brings you to my neck of the woods?"

Austin quickly realized that the woman he'd planned to seduce was turning the tables on him. Not that he minded having a willing counterpart, but if she wasn't careful, her provocative act was going to send him over the edge sooner than he'd anticipated. "I'm looking for a place to bunk down for the night," he drawled, struggling to maintain his composure when all he wanted to do was take this woman up against the wall, finesse be damned. "And I was hoping you could accommodate a lonesome cowboy."

Batting her lashes demurely at him, she skimmed her fingers over the swell of her breasts. Austin's mouth went dry as her nipples tightened.

A seductive smile added to her beguiling act. "Well, you're more than welcome to sleep in the stable with your horse."

He chuckled at her unexpected reply. "In that case, I guess I'm going to have to confess that I'm actually an outlaw seeking refuge, and I'll be taking you hostage." Making good on his threat, he moved into the entryway, closed the door behind him, and forced her up against the wall with the muscular heat of his body.

Her luminous brown eyes widened in mock fear and genuine excitement as she entwined her arms around his neck. "Dare I hope you'll be ravishing me?"

Dropping his duffel bag, he plowed his fingers into her

hair so he could lift her mouth to his—not that she was resisting much. "Didn't your parents ever warn you just how dangerous an outlaw could be?" he growled.

"Oh, yeah, they've tried, but I can't help my attraction to a man in chaps and spurs," she admitted, her voice dropping to a honeyed purr. She lifted her hips, encountering the thick length of his erection framed between the crotch of his chaps. "Especially an outlaw who has a weapon as impressive as yours. I hope you aren't afraid to use it."

A guttural groan ripped from his chest. He'd been hard for the past ten minutes, ever since she'd opened the door, but her teasing, arousing monologue increased the pressure in his groin to near pain. "Damn, but you're feisty."

She flashed him a sassy grin. "Shut up and kiss me, cowboy."

Not one to refuse such a tempting offer, he gave her exactly what she demanded—a hot, deep French kiss that quickly had them both wild for so much more. He lifted his mouth from hers long enough to pick up his duffel, then he swung her into his arms, swallowing her squeal of alarm as his lips closed over hers once again for another tongue-tangling kiss. Maneuvering her through the condo to the bedroom took effort, especially since she now had his face between her hands and was kissing him senseless. With every jangling step he took, her breathing deepened, and her urgency seemed to mount, matching the frenzied beat of his heart.

He found the bedroom minutes later, but not before taking a quick tour of her office, where Teddy breathlessly informed him they were in the wrong room—unless he wanted to use her desk. Tempted, but determined to make love to her properly this first time, he continued, stopping briefly in the hallway to readjust his hold on the woman in his arms while she placed damp, openmouthed kisses on his neck that made him weak in the knees. He bumped his hip against the dresser, muttered an oath that made her giggle, and blindly searched for her bed in the dark. Finally, his knees connected with something soft and wide, and he unceremoniously dropped her onto the mattress. She yelped in surprise, and he heard the springs creak as she bounced.

Setting the duffel close by, he switched on the lamp on the nightstand, illuminating the room, and Teddy, in a soft glow of light. She was sprawled on top of the floral comforter covering the bed, her blond hair a cloud of silk around her head, her eyes alight with awareness, and that scrap of nothing nightie up around her hips. He was certain the diaphanous panties barely covering her mound were designed to drive a man to primitive measures. He was nearly there.

Tipping the Stetson back on his head, he eyed those long, slender limbs of hers with unabashed male appreciation. "I think this is the part where I ravish you," he said wickedly.

A pretty shade of pink flushed her skin, and she tilted her head speculatively as her gaze once again took in his attire. "Why are you dressed up like this?" she asked, her voice as soft as the moonlight filtering in through the bedroom window.

"This last fantasy is for you, Teddy," he said, and knew by the slight catch to her breathing that she understood the significance of this final performance as *her* cowboy.

She stared at him in anticipation as he lifted a small recorder from his bag, put it on the nightstand, and hit play. Seconds later, the same upbeat, rockabilly tune he'd danced to for her birthday filled the silence of the night, the pulsing sound as provocative as the look darkening her eyes.

Spotting the Stetson he'd given her that same night, he retrieved it from the dresser, and settled it on her head, grinning at the luscious picture she made. "Merry Christmas, honey."

He straightened, intending to get the show on the road and give this woman a fantasy she'd never forget—and an incredible night that would hopefully change the course of their relationship. Rocking and rolling his hips to the rhythm of the country beat, he reached for the top snap on his western shirt to rip it open.

"Wait!" she blurted, holding up a hand to stop him.

He immediately ceased all movement, paralyzed with the unsettling possibility that she might be having second thoughts about them, about this.

Sitting up on her knees in front of him, she chewed on her lower lip uncertainly. "Would you be terribly disappointed if I undressed you, instead of you stripping for me?" Her voice quivered with an endearing hesitancy, then her chin lifted with that sassiness he was coming to adore. "I mean, after all, this is *my* fantasy."

He chuckled, unable to help himself. God, he loved how sexy and bold she was, and knew life with her would always be invigorating. "There's nothing that would please me more," he told her, a small part of his mind wondering how he'd be able to withstand such torment. "Where would you like to start?"

She crooked her finger at him. "Come a little closer."

The rowels on his boots chinked seductively as he did as she requested. Now it was her hips that swayed to the music, her hands that lifted to his chest. Gripping the material in her fists on either side of the pearl buttons, she ripped open his shirt.

A groan of pure pleasure rumbled in her throat as she smoothed her palms over the heat of his skin and explored to her heart's content, pushing him to the brink of madness. Following the light sprinkling of hair on his chest downward, she splayed a hand low on his taut belly and nudged him back a foot and stood.

With an intoxicating, feminine confidence that made him burn, she slid the tips of her fingers upward, flicking over his flattened nipples on her journey up to his shoulders, where she slowly dragged the shirt down his arms. And during this gradual striptease, when she had his hands tangled in cotton, she moved close and brushed her body against his to the beat of the music—her breasts, her belly, her thighs, all inflaming his senses.

His nostrils flared, and as soon as she tugged his shirt off and tossed it somewhere behind him, he caught her around the waist with one arm, slid a thigh between hers, and brought her flush to his hard length, trapping her arms between them.

She wasn't intimidated by his domination, or the fierce arousal pressing against her belly. "Hold your horses, cowboy," she whispered against his mouth, her gaze hot and eager for what was to come—albeit in her own sweet time. "This is my fantasy, and I'm not done yet."

Austin groaned, certain he'd never be able to hold out.

With her arms locked between them, her hand found the bulge tightening the front of his jeans. Shamelessly, she cupped the fullness in her palm, stroked him to the beat of the music as her own hips gyrated provocatively against his. Austin gritted his teeth as a shudder ripped through him. Heeding that fierce warning, he let her go the same moment her fingers hooked around the sides of his chaps and she gave a hard yank. Velcro tore apart, and with a triumphant grin, she flung the soft leather aside.

And from there, with each article of clothing she playfully removed from his body and tossed haphazardly in the room, from his cowboy boots with those spurs he'd worn just for her, to his jeans and briefs and then finally his Stetson, she totally captivated Austin, bringing warmth and laughter to a place deep within him that had been cold and lonely for too long. She was wicked, amusing, damn sexy, and everything he wanted in a woman.

Teddy stared breathlessly at the gorgeous, naked man standing in the middle of her bedroom—*her fantasy*. Austin was, in a word, *magnificent*. He was solidly aroused, all aggressive male, and she thrilled at the notion that she'd brought him to this.

Not quite ready to relinquish the heady rush of feminine power coursing through her veins, she circled him, languidly caressing the firm slope of his back, his tight buttocks, and planting teasing, biting kisses along his throat and chest. Closing her eyes, she slid lower, until the very male essence of him brushed her lips—and heard a rough, strangled sound catch in his throat that was half pain, half pleasure.

Reckless excitement curled through her, settling in the pit of her belly, spreading outward. Eager to taste him in a way she'd never experienced before, she closed her mouth intimately over him, indulging in the smooth, velvety texture of his skin, the virile heat of him sliding along her tongue...

His entire body instinctively bucked toward her, and he sucked in a swift, shocked breath. His hands lifted, knocking the Stetson on her head to the floor. His long fingers tangled in her hair, at first guiding her untutored, but very erotic offering, then in a frantic attempt to pull her away.

Swearing viciously, he dragged her back up again. She

caught a quick glimpse of the hot need glowing in the depths of his gaze before he fluidly, effortlessly, turned her, banded his strong arms around her waist, and tucked her backside against the front of his body.

She gasped, her heart slamming against her ribs. It was like being surrounded by fire...so much heat, raw and intense. Flames licked along her back, her thighs, and that out-of-control wildfire even found its way to the tips of her breasts, and her belly, where he'd splayed one of his hands to keep her bottom nestled close to his groin. The dresser mirror in front of them gave her a perfect view of their intimate position, enabling her to see the flush on her skin, the exhilaration in her eyes. The alluring sight aroused her, made her pulse flutter anxiously for what was to come.

He buried his face against the side of her neck, and she shivered as his harsh breathing branded her skin. Gradually, his mouth charted a warm, damp path to her ear. "I feel at a distinct disadvantage here, darlin'," he drawled in a low voice that rumbled along her nerve endings. "I'm buck naked, and you've got way too many clothes on."

She wanted to laugh at his attempt at levity, but all she could think of was his hands sliding on her skin, his body easing into hers, and the wild ride he'd give her. "Then take them off," she dared impudently.

A warm chuckle reverberated against her neck. "Yes, ma'am." Sliding his hands beneath the hem of her gown, he slowly drew the soft material up and over her head, and tossed it somewhere in the room, leaving her clad in just her panties. She felt no embarrassment, only an acute desire for him to touch her as intimately as she'd touched him.

Somehow, he knew. As his gaze met hers in the mirror, he lifted his hands and cupped her swollen breasts in his palms, rasped his thumbs across her nipples until they were stiff and aching. Biting back a soft moan, she pressed her hands to the sides of his thighs, rolled her head back onto his shoulder, and arched her body more fully into his hands. He nuzzled her neck, stroked his fingers down her trembling belly and teased her through the damp, silky material of her panties until a whimper escaped her and her knees threatened to buckle.

Turning in his arms, she sought his mouth with hers, and he didn't hesitate to give her the kind of kiss she craved. No more teasing. No more gentle humor. Just intense passion and sizzling desire. She wanted it all, and she wanted it with him.

While his mouth consumed hers, and his tongue delved deep, he moved with her toward the bed. The back of her knees hit the edge, and he urged her down upon the mattress, pushing aside the Stetson that had landed there earlier so she could lie down, though he didn't join her. Instead, he dragged her panties over her slim hips and down her long limbs. Then he leisurely kissed his way up first one leg, then the other, stopping to explore every erogenous zone with his lips and tongue and the soft strum of his fingers.

The seductive journey took him all the way up to her quivering thighs, where he nipped the sensitive flesh with his teeth, then soothed the bites with long, slow laps of his tongue. He moved on to her belly, swirled his tongue in her navel, then closed his mouth over her breast and suckled the tender flesh until her entire body throbbed for that mystical release...

"Austin, please," she begged.

He lifted his head, a wholly wicked grin slashing across his features. "But I'm not done ravishing you, darlin'.

Any cowboy worth his chaps isn't gonna leave his lady so worked up."

Just when she thought she couldn't stand any more of the dizzying sensations, he slipped down on the bed, used his palms to nudge her thighs apart, and claimed her in the most intimate kind of caress of all. His fingers filled her, sliding deeply. The heat of his mouth engulfed her. And the silky, rhythmic glide of his tongue sent her soaring straight into the realms of bliss.

Her release was swift and powerful, her cries lusty and unabashed. Her fingers twisted in the covers in an attempt to keep her grounded, but she flew apart anyway, reveling in the luxurious climax that seemed to go on and on. And when she finally tumbled back to earth, panting for breath, her body limp, she opened her eyes to find Austin standing by the side of the bed, sheathing himself in a condom.

"Wow," she whispered, awed by her body's ability to melt and surrender at Austin's whim—first in his car earlier, and now. "Twice in one night. Incredible."

Finished with the necessary protection, he knelt between her spread knees, then moved over her, settling himself between her still-quivering thighs. Bracing his forearms on either side of her head so they were face-to-face, he allowed a devilish grin to claim his lips. "Darlin', we're going for a third."

Her pulse quickened, and leaped again when his thick sex slid against her damp cleft, the velvety tip of his erection finding the entrance to her body. She was primed and ready, but he didn't penetrate more than a teasing inch. "I couldn't..."

"Oh, yeah, you can." His fingers wove through her hair, cradling her head in his big hands as he eased his chest against her breasts, crushing her with the delicious weight and heat of his body. His dark green eyes glittered with hunger, and powerful emotion that seemed to touch her soul. "And this time, I want to hear my name on your lips when you come..."

And with that demand, he filled her with one smooth, hard thrust. She gasped as her body stretched to accommodate him. He let out a low, animal groan as her sleek, inner muscles clenched him tight. Instinctively, she wrapped her legs around his hips and arched into him. He growled in response to her seductive move and surged against her, sliding deeper still.

She saw his restraint in the tight clenching of his jaw, felt it in the taut line of his body. Sliding her hands down his muscled back and over his firm buttocks, she urged him to take what he wanted and give in to those primal desires. "This ride is all yours, cowboy," she murmured in a husky whisper.

He shook his head, humor dancing in those smoky eyes of his. "Ladies first," he said, male arrogance tinging his deep voice. "I insist."

She laughed lightly, but the playful sound ebbed into a moan when he bent his head and captured her lips with his, kissing her in the same erotic manner he made love to her. He had a point to prove, and set out to demonstrate the wonders of a female body, and just how well he knew hers.

He continued to kiss her, ruthlessly maintaining a steady rhythm designed to push her closer to that sublime ecstasy. Her heart raced, and incredibly, with each slow, measured stroke, each primal lunge, she felt the gradual building of yet another climax. Intense pleasure coiled inside her, urging her to move with him, toward the promise of something lush and wild and spectacular.

She was close...so, so close.

He lifted his head, sliding his mouth from hers to watch her expression. His gaze locked with hers, demanding and fiery. There was no way she could hide anything from him, he wouldn't allow it. He coaxed not only her physical surrender, but an emotional one, too...and she found the feelings swirling within her thrilling, arousing and terrifying, because she'd never given a man what Austin silently asked for...her complete acquiescence, heart, body and soul.

"Let it go, baby," he rasped, as if he understood her fears. "I'll catch you when you fall."

Helpless to deny him, she closed her mind to everything, ceasing to exist past the feel of him moving in her, over her...and then it happened, a blinding rush of sensation that stole her breath and spilled through her like liquid fire.

The orgasm was so intense, she grasped his shoulders for fear of flying apart. And just as she reached the peak and her body convulsed with the exquisite, sensual gratification, she gave him what he'd ultimately wanted.

"*Austin...*" she moaned huskily, raggedly.

A satisfied light glimmered in his eyes. "Yeah, just like that..."

In a series of hard, swift strokes he thrust into her, and as she watched him toss back his head and give himself over to his own violent climax, she realized she'd gone and done something utterly foolish.... Something that would only lead to a wealth of heartache for her, false expectations from her parents, and a string of disappointments for the man who'd possessed her body so thoroughly.

She'd fallen hard and deep for Austin McBride.

STANDING BY the side of the bed, Austin stared down at the woman sprawled on her stomach amidst the tangle of

sheets and blankets, unable to help the lazy smile tipping
his mouth, or the warm inner glow chasing away the chill
still clinging to his skin from his predawn quest through
the misty, rainy morning to find Teddy a special Christmas surprise. No easy feat, considering every tree lot he'd
driven to had sold out the night before.

Finally, his persistence had paid off. He'd found a lone,
solitary tree in an abandoned lot, a scrawny five-foot
Douglas fir with a broken limb and a crooked trunk that
wobbled haphazardly on the wooden base it had been
nailed to. Knowing how effortlessly Teddy could trans-
form such imperfection, he'd claimed the tree. While he
was trying to secure the five-foot shrub to the top of the
Mustang, it had started to rain, a cold drizzle that gradually soaked through his shirt and jeans.

The slight discomfort would be worth seeing Teddy's
face light up with joy when she saw her surprise. Her very
own Christmas tree, to decorate as she pleased, and to
share with him. This year, she wouldn't be alone on
Christmas morning. This year, he'd give her every reason
to celebrate.

He had nothing to wrap and put beneath the tree for
her. The thought had crossed his mind on the drive back
to her place, but he'd decided that he wanted to give
Teddy something more personal than a tangible gift,
something precious and priceless, something all the
money in the world couldn't buy. Something she was in
dire need of, even if she didn't realize it yet.

His love.

Yeah, he loved her. The emotion had snuck up on him
when he'd least expected it, stealing into his heart and
making him realize he needed this feisty, stubborn, too-
independent woman in his life. He wanted a wife to come

home to at night and share his life with, and he wanted children to bring love and laughter to a home that hadn't experienced much merriment since his parents had died. He imagined all those things, and more...and in every mental picture that projected in his mind, Teddy played a central part in his future.

His feelings for her were crazy, nothing he'd ever prepared himself for, yet there was no denying what he felt for her exceeded anything he'd ever experienced. And despite their different backgrounds and her parents' uncertainties about him, the only person's opinion that mattered to him was Teddy's.

He knew that needing someone didn't come easily to Teddy, but he harbored enough confidence to believe her feelings for him were just as strong as his were for her, which, at the very least, gave them a solid foundation to build on. He'd seen the emotion in her eyes when he'd made love to her last night, the uninhibited way she'd responded to him told a tale of its own. But he'd also sensed her uncertainty after that first joining, felt the barest hint of reservation. And he wasn't going to give her time to come up with any regrets.

Luckily for him, she was easily distracted. He'd kept her mouth and hands and mind as busy as his own. He'd fanned the flames of desire all over again, taking her in possessive, erotic ways that had at first shocked Teddy, then incited her to new, feverish heights. They'd made good use of the box of condoms he'd brought, and in the dark hours of the night he hoped he'd managed to strip away a few layers of that frustrating reserve.

She let out a soft, slumberous sigh and shifted on the mattress, stretching out more fully on her belly and sprawling those gorgeous legs of hers across most of the bed. He couldn't help but grin. If he'd still been lying be-

side her, she would have kicked him right off the edge.
The woman was a bed-hog.

The covers wrapped loosely around her slender hips
and tangled around her shapely legs, leaving the smooth
slope of her back bare to his gaze, and hinting at the soft,
warm nakedness beneath the sheet. Her arms were folded
around a pillow, her face buried in the softness, and the
slight curve to her body afforded him a glimpse of one
full, pale breast.

Not so surprisingly, sexual heat surged through his
body, settling into an insistent throb in his groin. Amaz-
ingly, he grew full and heavy beneath his cold, wet briefs
and the denim molding to his hips and thighs. Welcoming
the rush of warmth and anticipating the greater heat of
Teddy's body, he stripped his damp T-shirt over his head
and dropped it to the floor. He toed off his shoes, tugged
off his soaked socks, and struggled to push the wet denim
over his hips and down his legs. Completely naked, and
fully aroused, he slipped beneath the covers and moved
toward Teddy.

The moment his chilled flesh touched hers she gasped
and came awake, her head lifting from the pillow. She
looked disoriented, her tousled hair falling over her face,
her eyes hazy. Before she could turn around or scramble
away, he aligned his body over hers from behind, pressed
her back down on the mattress, and pulled the blankets
up around them.

"Austin?" she said, her voice husky and a little bewildered.

He dragged his open mouth along her jaw, nuzzled the
warm, fragrant hollow of neck, tasting her skin with his
lips and the touch of his tongue. "'Morning," he murmured, his rumbly voice low and intimate in the shadowed gray before dawn. The soft, rhythmic pitter-patter

of rain against the window added to the lazy, sensual morning.

She released a drowsy, complacent "Mmm" as he caressed along the indentation of her waist with his hands, then shivered when he slipped his palms along her ribs and finally tucked his chilled hands between her breasts and the mattress to warm them.

She sucked in a swift breath as her nipples beaded against his icy palms. "You're freezing," she complained as another shudder ran though her, though she made no move to push him off her.

Nudging her thighs apart, he settled between that warm, welcoming harbor. "I won't be for long," he whispered, gently rubbing his stubbled cheek along her smooth shoulder. His damp hair brushed her skin, and he felt her shiver again.

"And you're wet," she said, her voice filled with confusion.

"I think that's my line." He rolled his hips forward, gliding his hot, male flesh along her slick, feminine cleft, proving his point.

She laughed huskily, and wriggled her bottom beneath him, impatiently seeking the deeper contact he planned to give her in his own sweet time. She drew a deep breath, and released it slowly. "You smell like rain, and pine."

"Imagine that." Smiling at the puzzled note to her voice, he eased a hand away from her breast, slid his flattened palm down her belly, and threaded his way through silky, damp curls to a greater fire, a more desperate need. Sultry desire drenched his fingertips the moment he touched her.

She whimpered beneath him, and he groaned, the heaviness and hunger inside him intensifying. "Ah, you feel so damn good, Teddy," he breathed. Sinking deeper into her lush heat, he plied that tiny nub of flesh, giving her nothing but pleasure. Her breathing quickened, and he had the fleeting thought that he might be crushing her with his weight. "Am I too heavy for you?" he murmured against her ear.

"Nnnnooo," she moaned, her legs parting wider for his touch, while her fingers gripped the pillow. She turned her head to glance back at him, but got caught up in the tremors shimmering through her body. He watched her eyes roll back in ecstasy, her lips part, and a long, keening cry rip from her throat as she gave herself over to the erotic sensations.

Satisfaction swelled in his chest, and he continued to stroke her, slowly, exquisitely, reverently, until the last bit of rapture ebbed—reveling in the fact that this time, she didn't even try to temper the emotional climax.

Her unconditional response turned him on, humbled him, even. Wanting to give the same in return, he dragged his palms from beneath her, found her hands, and laced their fingers together at the side of her head. "Lift your hips for me, Teddy," he rasped near her ear, desperate to be inside her.

She accommodated his request without hesitation, and he slid into her with a sleek, heavy glide, surrounding her with flesh that was no longer chilled, but now burned with the wild need to possess her in the most elemental way possible.

Mutual groans coalesced, and his hips began pumping harder, faster. Her fingers tightened around his, and she whispered his name, over and over, a sweet, drugging litany that dragged him deeper into the flames.

The sensations crashing over him stole his breath. The powerful emotions he felt for this woman touched his heart, overwhelming him, sending him careening straight over the edge of control. Burying deep, he arched against her and rode with the most excruciating pleasure he'd ever known.

11

SIGHING CONTENTEDLY, Teddy draped her leg over Austin's and rested her head in the crook of his shoulder, unable to think of a nicer way to wake up in the morning—making love to an exceptionally sexual, virile man who was as generous with her pleasure as he was greedy about taking his own satisfaction. The delicious, satiated glow spreading through her was something she could get used to.

Sex had never been a necessity for her, certainly not something she'd given much importance to in her pursuit to establish her career, but she quickly realized it was a matter of making love to the right man. She couldn't get enough of Austin, the excitement of his kisses, the thrill of his touch, and even the sexy way he looked at her that could make her smolder and burn until he extinguished those internal flames of desire.

Their sexual compatibility and sizzling attraction was a win-win situation, and though her startling realization last night had scared her on an emotional level, she'd put her feelings for Austin into perspective during the night and decided to handle the situation like any other independent woman would. She'd have an affair with Austin. A simple, undemanding relationship that wouldn't interfere with the goals she'd worked so hard to achieve, or threaten the unrestricted life-style she'd finally established for herself. A no-strings tryst that wouldn't give

Austin any false illusions about a forever kind of future together. No promises. No long-term commitment.

Satisfied with her plan, she lifted her head to look at Austin, furrowing her fingers in the soft, curly hair on his chest. His eyes were closed, and he looked exhausted, completely wiped out. And totally gorgeous with dark morning stubble lining his lean jaw. She thought about that roughness against her neck and shoulders during their last erotic interlude, and her skin tingled with renewed awareness. Slowly, she skimmed her palm down to his belly, slipped her hand beneath the sheet draped over his hips, and curled her warm fingers over his semi-erect shaft.

He groaned, and grabbing her wrist, he pulled her hand back up so it rested over the steady beating of his heart. "Have mercy, woman. I need a little time to recuperate," he muttered, eyes still closed.

She laughed softly, and took pity on his poor, abused body. "Okay, I'll give you ten minutes, and if you're still being uncooperative, I'll just have to climb on top and straddle you while you're sleeping."

The corner of his mouth twitched. "You're a shameless hussy."

"It's all your fault," she said, reaching up to run her fingers through Austin's still-damp hair, which brought to mind how cold and wet he'd been when he'd slipped into bed with her just a little while ago. "So tell me, why were you all wet?"

"As you can see, it's raining outside," he said, his voice a deep, rumbling murmur.

She glanced toward the window, watching rivulets of water run down the pane. The soft sound of rain outside soothed her. "Hmm, so it is." But that didn't really answer her question, so she rephrased it. "What were you doing out *in* the rain?"

The eye closest to her opened halfway, enough for her to glimpse feigned exasperation. "You're not going to let me sleep, are you?"

"Nope." Smiling at his poor attempt to appear annoyed, she stacked her hands on his chest and rested her chin on top. "What were you doing out in the rain?" she repeated.

Both eyes opened, brilliant green and full of mischief now. "Getting your Christmas present."

Her heart flip-flopped in her chest at that surprising announcement. It *was* Christmas morning, and the last thing she expected was a gift from Austin, especially when she hadn't gotten him anything in return. "You didn't have to do that."

"I wanted to." He brushed a strand of hair off her cheek, his touch infinitely tender, the look in his eyes just as adoring.

The swell of emotion she experienced for this man at that moment terrified her, and she quickly suppressed it. "What store would be open on Christmas, at six in the morning?"

He lifted a dark eyebrow. "Well, Ms. Skeptical, why don't we just go find out?"

Like a giddy kid on Christmas morning, Teddy sprang from the bed and grabbed the long, cotton robe hanging on the hook behind the bathroom door. Slipping into it, she came back to the bedroom and found Austin sitting on the side of the bed, still naked, and frowning at the garments on the floor.

He glanced up at her. "My clothes are all wet, except for my costume, and I'm afraid those chaps might be a little drafty."

She laughed, though the thought of all that gorgeous masculinity framed in nothing but leather chaps made her pulse quicken. "But oh so sexy," she said breathlessly.

"I'd be happy to oblige that fantasy later, darlin'," he drawled huskily. "But right now, I'd prefer to keep the important parts warm."

She tightened the sash on her robe, and extended an offer before she lost the nerve. "Maybe you ought to leave a few extra changes of clothes here."

His gaze held hers for an immeasurable moment, dark and searching. "Maybe," he said, his tone completely noncommittal.

Not wanting to delve any deeper into that subject at the moment, she rummaged through her dresser drawers, withdrawing a pair of light pink drawstring sweat shorts she wore around the house. Turning, she held them out to Austin. "This should work, for now. I know they look small, but they stretch, and they're comfortable."

His expression turned doubtful, but without any other options available, he went ahead and stepped into the snug shorts. Sure enough, the fabric stretched to accommodate his muscular form. The soft pink cotton molded to everything male about him, from his lean hips and tight buttocks, to the masculine bulge between his hard thighs.

"Wow, the color pink really suits you," she teased.

He propped his hands on his hips and glared. "I'm sure your parents would be thrilled to find out I wear women's clothing."

She smothered a giggle. "My lips are sealed." Grabbing his hand, she tugged him toward the bedroom door. "So, where's this surprise?"

"In the living room."

She headed in that direction, but before they reached the end of the short hallway, he stopped her, turning her to face him. Uncertainty flickered in the depth of his eyes, touching a chord deep within her.

"It's really not much, but it's something I hope might become a tradition."

His words puzzled her, but she didn't have much time to ponder them. He asked her to close her eyes, and once she did, he rested his hands lightly on her shoulders and guided her into the living room. The scent of pine added to her bewilderment.

"Merry Christmas, sweetheart," he said from behind her, his words warm and heartfelt.

Teddy opened her eyes, and gasped at the sight of the Christmas tree sitting in the corner of the room, crooked and fractured in places, but its spirit not broken. The tree was nothing grand, a misfit among Douglas firs, but the sentiment behind Austin's gesture transcended grandeur. The lengths he'd gone through to offer her this special gift exceeded anything anyone had ever done for her.

"It's all yours, to decorate as you please," he said, pressing a soft kiss against her hair. "And you're not alone this year. You can share it with me."

Realizing he must have overheard the conversation she'd had with Jordan about her childhood, her throat tightened and tears burned the back of her eyes.

It's really not much, but it's something I hope might become a tradition.

Now his words made sense, the meaning behind his remark teeming with assumptions...and complications. "Tradition" implied something lasting, tied up with commitment, and the future. A custom passed on from year, to year, and shared with loved ones.

Oh, Lord. While she wanted to maintain a casual relationship with Austin, he'd sailed headlong into forbidden territory, making subtle insinuations she wasn't near ready to face.

Feeling suffocated, and unable to think straight, she pasted on a smile, and turned to face him. "This is great," she said way too brightly. "Let's decorate it. I'll make some popcorn and we can string it and put it on the tree."

She started toward the kitchen, but he caught her arm, stopping her. His gaze flickered over her face, and she desperately tried not to let her fear show.

"This isn't everything, Teddy." His tone was so gentle, she wanted to weep.

"It's certainly enough," she said, the double meaning escaping on choked laughter.

He hesitated, his own expression momentarily uncertain. Then his gaze cleared, and his fingers slid from her upper arm down to her hand, which he held loosely in his palm. "I love you, Teddy."

Her stomach sank, and she visibly flinched at the words, so sweet, so powerful...so smothering. She shook her head in denial. "No, please, don't."

"Don't love you?" he asked, surprise etching his features. "It's too late, because I'm already too far gone. Don't say the words? I have to, because I want you to know how serious I am about you. About us."

She pulled her hand from his. "This is too much, too fast..."

The beginnings of a frown appeared on his face, exposing a niggling of concern. "I know you told me that you don't have time for a relationship right now, but I'd think after the past week, hell, after last night, you'd make time. What we have together is more than just an itch we both need to scratch."

Her face flushed, yet she couldn't shake the feeling of being smothered. Of becoming just as accommodating as her sisters-in-law, and her mother. "Why can't we just have an affair, and enjoy our time together for as long as it lasts?"

He jammed his hands on his hips, his eyes darkening to a fierce shade of green. "So, you want to use me for sex?"

His harsh voice sent a trickle of uneasiness skidding down her spine. She'd obviously provoked him, but admitting the truth was far better than leading him astray with false promises. "I enjoy being with you, Austin, but I've got a job to think about, and a committed relationship would demand more time than I have to give right now." Her words sounded selfish to her own ears but, dammit, she cherished her independence, the freedom to come and go as she pleased, without answering to anyone.

Her mental assurance lacked a certain conviction she refused to analyze.

Irritation tightened his jaw. "I've got my own business to run, and I'm not demanding anything more from you than you're willing to give. I was hoping we could meet somewhere in the middle."

She rubbed her forehead wearily, knowing from experience that it rarely worked out so compatibly. Relationships turned demanding in time, and eventually destructive. She shook her head, feeling torn and confused, but ultimately holding on to the belief that balancing a career and relationship wasn't for her. "I...can't," she whispered achingly.

"Why not?" he persisted.

His direct question stirred up many answers, and a whole lot of resentments she'd kept tucked away for so many years. Turning away, she moved deeper into the living room, away from the vibrant heat of Austin's body, and attempted to explain her reasons the best she could. "It's taken me years to finally become my own person, to finally break free of my family's influence. Ever since I was a little girl, my parents have had certain expectations of me. As a teenager, I was groomed to be a 'lady,' went to every country-club dance there was and dated 'respectable' boys. And when I graduated from high school, my mother set me up with an endless string of potential husband prospects. Every guy I went out with came from an affluent family, and usually after the second or third date my mother was hinting at a wedding. That's when I broke things off with the guy I was dating, before my mother had the chance to throw an engagement party."

Standing by the Christmas tree, she reached out and tentatively touched one of the limbs, trying not to let the sentiment behind Austin's gift get the best of her. She'd never known a man so sweet, so selfless, yet her misgivings wouldn't allow her to accept what he so generously offered.

Swallowing the huge knot forming in her throat, she continued. "All I wanted was to go to college and pursue a career in graphic design, which I loved. All I got from my parents was nothing but grief, because I was too focused on a career when there was no need for me to work. They disapproved of my choices, and ever since the age of eighteen, I've been nothing but a disappointment to them." She glanced over her shoulder at Austin, meeting his gaze and praying he wouldn't hate her too badly once this was over. "You saw what I went through last night."

Something in his eyes softened, and he stepped toward her. "Teddy—"

She held up a hand to ward him off, wanting him to know everything. One touch from him, and she'd lose all train of thought. "Then there was Bartholomew Winston, who was, of course, handpicked by my father and came with my mother's full approval. He was a banker like his father and grandfather before him, came from old money, and was wealthy enough to impress my parents. After a few months of dating Bart, I finally gave in to the pressure. I had a ring on my finger, a wedding date set, and china patterns all picked out."

"Did you love him?" Austin asked, that question seemingly important to him.

"No, I didn't love him," she admitted, a sad smile touching her mouth. "I cared for him, and I thought that was enough, because he was the first guy who understood and accepted my goals." She'd learn later that his approval was all an illusion, a way to temporarily appease her. "For the first time in longer than I could remember, my mother and I had a decent relationship. She was in her glory making wedding plans, and I tried to convince myself that I could be happy." She couldn't contain the self-deprecating laugh that bubbled out of her. "About three months before the wedding, my parents sat Bart and I down and told me that now that I was getting married to a very prominent man, I should give up this foolishness of having a career. Certainly I couldn't be a proper wife if I was busy working outside the mansion," she added sarcastically.

He stood there, too far away, arms crossed over his wide chest, watching her with unfathomable eyes, listening, waiting. He appeared so patient, so understanding, yet there was something in his stance that promised something a bit more charged.

She drew a deep breath, and tightened the sash on her robe, not to keep the lapels together, but in an attempt to keep herself from falling apart. "Bart agreed with my parents, when I thought all along he understood how important being a graphic designer was to me. But he changed his tune, insisting that he wouldn't have a wife who worked when there was no need for her to do so. And so I insisted that he take his ring back and find a more submissive female who wanted to be his keeper."

Dragging a hand through her disheveled hair, she inwardly winced as she remembered the fiasco that erupted in her father's study after her very indelicate declaration. "My parents totally freaked out, but I'd never felt so liberated as I did in that moment. And from then on, I vowed that I'd depend on no one but myself. I moved out of the house, much to my parents' dismay, and I've been supporting myself ever since. I've totally disgraced them, but the move bolstered my confidence." She watched Austin slowly move closer, and her chin rose in a stubborn show of bravado. Unfortunately, her insecurities couldn't be so easily masked. "I like my independence. I've struggled for it. I've earned it, and I don't want to give it up."

Very gently, he used his thumb and forefinger and lowered her chin back down, as if silently telling her she had no reason to be defensive with him. "Who said anything about giving it up?" Before she could issue a response, he continued. "What makes you think you can't have a relationship *and* a career? What makes you think I'd ever try and stifle you like your parents have tried to do?"

His barrage of questions made her head spin. His nearness made her long to put her arms around his neck, cling to his strength, and forget about every one of her doubts. "Because that's what ultimately happens! I've been through it personally, and I've seen my brothers do it to each of their wives—"

He scoffed, a harsh sound that cut through her protests. "Oh, you'd be surprised, Teddy. If I learned anything last night, it's that your sisters-in-law are hardly the submissive types. They let your brothers think they have the upper hand and put on a good show for your mother and father, but every one of them is an independent, self-sufficient woman who seems to have found an equal balance with her husband."

His insightful view astounded her, and left her speechless.

He took advantage of her wide-eyed stare. "You have nothing to prove to me, Teddy," he said. "Nothing at all. I love you just the way you are, stubborn, independent and determined to grasp that promotion you want so badly. And I'd never do anything to change the person you are, or interfere with what's important to you."

She heard his words, and really wanted to believe them, but couldn't stem the rise of panic that flooded her...a deep-rooted fear that his understanding would wane in time.

She thought into the future, to where a committed relationship with Austin would lead, and her doubts were confirmed. "But you want a wife, and babies."

"Yeah, I do," he admitted. "Eventually."

"I don't want that," she said, issuing the denial out of self-preservation.

"Don't you?" His deep voice was calm and soothing, but his eyes pierced her with a perception that shook her to the depths of her soul.

She paced away from him, the intensity of her feelings for Austin deluging her with more unsettling thoughts. Her deep longing for him seemed to eclipse her lifelong need for independence and made her wonder what her life would be like if she eventually married Austin and gave him the babies he wanted.

And that's where everything became a jumbled, conflicting mess in her mind. She'd been taught that women were supposed to be complacent, dutiful wives, and when babies came along, women stayed at home, falling into a maternal role that didn't include the career Teddy had spent years working toward.

Dread balled in her stomach, overriding sense or reason. "No, I don't want that," she forced herself to say, and tried her best to believe those words. Sinking into the cushions of the couch, she beseeched Austin with her gaze. "All this has taken me by surprise. I wasn't expecting to fall for you. And I don't think I can be what you ultimately need in your life." The statement came out as a tight, aching whisper.

His mouth stretched into a grim line. "You're not even willing to try."

"I'm willing to give you what I can." She hated the uncertain quiver in her voice. Hated even more the fear that ruled her emotions.

"A no-strings affair," he said, his tone flat.

Right now, it was all she could offer him. "Yes."

"No way. It's not enough." His expression turned angry. "I've been used like that before, and I won't be anyone's part-time plaything again."

Hearing the heated condemnation in his voice, and suspecting he, too, had been played for a fool in the past, she regarded him cautiously. "What are you talking about?"

"The last relationship I was in, if you could even call it that, was with a woman who was out for a good time, and I was it. Her name was Diane, and she was a Fantasy for Hire customer. Just like you, she was looking for a personal fantasy."

Teddy's heart sank as she realized the correlation between her own behavior and this other woman's. Beyond Austin's anger, she also heard the hurt in his deep voice, and realized that this other woman had trampled on his emotions and had given him a few insecurities of his own.

"She used me, Teddy, and when the affair came down to something more serious for me, she blew me off." Tension bunched the muscles across his chest and in his arms as he stood on the other side of the coffee table. "Bottom line, I wasn't good enough for her, and the life she led. Not on a permanent basis anyway."

She winced at the lash of his words, and the bitterness seeping into his tone. "I'm sorry," she said, her voice tight and aching.

"Yeah, me too." His cold gaze held hers relentlessly. "So no, I don't do convenient affairs, Teddy. I need some kind of commitment when I'm serious about a woman. No matter how old-fashioned it may seem, when I fall in love, I'm an all-or-nothing kind of guy. And I expect the same from the woman I'm involved with."

Her throat closed up, making speech impossible. His rare declaration of fidelity and devotion was what women dreamed of, and Teddy's heart swelled with so many regrets, so many fears...and the overwhelming need to believe him, and accept his precious offering. The upheaval of emotions swamped her, pulling her in two different directions.

Letting out a low sigh of defeat, he headed for the hallway that led to her bedroom—to gather up his things, she suspected—then stopped before disappearing. "And just for the record, Teddy, I've never told another woman that I was in love with her. You're the first, and I didn't make the declaration lightly."

She closed her eyes, listening to the rustling sounds drifting from down the hall, and tried to convince herself that it was best that things ended now, instead of when the relationship became more complicated. More demanding.

Her heart twisted unmercifully, rejecting the convenient excuse she desperately tried to cling to. Emotionally, she was already over her head—and the realization was alarming.

He returned to the living room minutes later, changed into his damp clothes, duffel bag in hand. "You're still hanging on to the fantasy, Teddy," he said, his gaze uncompromising as it held hers. "I'm offering you the real thing, and I won't accept anything less from you, either."

And then he was gone. As the silence and solitude she'd always cherished surrounded her, hot tears scalded her eyes. Seconds ticked into minutes, which turned into hours as she sat on the couch and stared at the Christmas tree Austin had bought for her, to share with her. Yet she'd pushed him out of her life, so determined to preserve her independence...so afraid to trust him with her heart.

"ARE YOU SURE I can't convince you to join Brenda and me for a drink at the Frisco Bay?" Laura asked, her concerned voice attempting to cajole Teddy into accepting the invitation.

"I'm sure." Teddy appreciated her friend's attempt to cheer her up, but there were too many memories of Austin at the Frisco Bay, and she just wasn't up to making polite conversation when her heart ached like nothing she'd ever experienced before.

It had been a week and a half since Christmas morning, when Austin had walked out of her life. She hadn't heard from him, not that she'd expected to after the angry way they'd parted. She'd spent the holiday weekend by herself, alone and lonely and wallowing in misery. The tree in her living room had remained undecorated, yet she couldn't bring herself to remove it from the condo, either.

She'd refused the New Year's Eve parties Laura and

Brenda had invited her to, feeling as though she had little to celebrate. Her parents had invited her and Austin over for New Year's Day brunch at the house, hoping to "get to know Austin better," since it seemed the two of them were serious about each other. Teddy declined that gracious offer with a convenient fib that she had other plans. She didn't have the heart to tell her mother that Austin was no longer a part of her life.

And after she'd hung up the phone, Teddy recognized the irony of her parents accepting Austin, even if it was on a tentative level, when she'd been the one to judge him so harshly.

Pushing that awful thought aside, she reached for a file on her desk and resumed her conversation with Laura. "I've got a proposal to finish up here at work," she said, pulling out the first draft copy of a resort brochure. "So I'll be here late tonight. You and Brenda go and have a good time."

"All right," Laura reluctantly agreed. "Hey, isn't tomorrow the day you find out if you get the senior graphic design promotion?"

Teddy found she couldn't even summon a small bout of enthusiasm over what once had been her sole ambition. "Yeah. There's a board meeting first thing in the morning. I should know by noon."

"Well, good luck, and keep me and Brenda posted."

Teddy managed a small smile, grateful for her friends' support. "Thanks, I will."

Hanging up the phone, she continued working on the brochure, making notes for narrative, and jotting down ideas for what she thought would make for an attractive, trifold advertisement. She welcomed the diversion—it kept thoughts of Austin at bay.

It was a little after 6:00 p.m., and outside her office she

could hear other employees leaving for the evening. The building grew quiet, except for the occasional hum of the copier being used by an ambitious employee working late like herself, or the ring of the outer telephone that someone else picked up. Another hour, she decided, and she'd pack up her work and head home, though the thought of entering her condo made her dread the lonely, solitary night ahead. It no longer seemed to matter that she'd once cherished the privacy and freedom that came with being an unattached woman.

"Trying to make a last-minute impression on me?"

Louden's sly voice slithered down Teddy's spine, and she glanced up to find her boss standing in the doorway to her office. "No, I'm trying to do my job and meet my current deadline. I'm sure you've made up your mind by now who will get the promotion."

Very casually, he entered the room, closing the door behind him. Her heart gave a distinct thump in her chest, and uneasiness congealed in her belly.

His pale gaze flickered over her silk blouse, then rose to her eyes again as he moved closer to her desk. "I submit my final choice tomorrow morning, *before* the board meeting begins. It's still not too late for me to put you at the top of the list." His insinuation rang clear—as of this moment, she wasn't his top candidate for the position. "How about dinner tonight?"

Feeling very uncomfortable being alone with Louden in her office, she stood and reached for her briefcase, deciding it was time to pack up and leave. "I don't think so. Austin is expecting me home shortly."

"Cut the pretense, Teddy," he said in a light, mocking tone that was at odds with the ominous glint in his eyes.

Her pulse leaped in apprehension. Trying to keep calm,

she gathered important files and stacked them in her briefcase. "I have no idea what you're talking about."

Bracing his hands on the desk across from her, he leaned in close. "He's a stripper," he said, his gaze sparkling with the trump card he'd just played.

A cold chill tingled along the surface of her skin, and her belly tightened with tension. She let none of her anxiety show. "Excuse me?" she asked, infusing her voice with a credible amount of bewilderment.

A slow, insidious smile curved his thin lips as he straightened. "Austin McBride is a stripper, a fantasy for hire, or in your case, an escort for hire who received a higher price than I'd ever demand for services rendered."

He knew too much, and she had no idea how Louden had discovered the truth about Austin. She watched him circle her desk, like a predatory animal closing in for the final victory, and snapped the locks closed on her briefcase.

"Aren't you the least bit curious how I know about Austin?" he asked. "Janet mentioned to me that she thought your boyfriend looked familiar at the Christmas party, and then it dawned on her where she'd seen him before...dressed as a cop, one who stripped for a living. Needless to say, I found that extremely interesting, and while you were at lunch today I found a business card and a receipt for a thousand dollars for 'services rendered' in your desk drawer."

White-hot fury filled her, and she turned to face Louden—who stood way too close for her comfort. "You went through my things?"

He shrugged, as if invading her privacy didn't violate a serious code of ethics.

Months of enduring Louden's tactics finally got the best of her. Fists clenching at her sides, she met his gaze challengingly, and let her temper boil over. "You had no right!"

He merely smiled, looking pleased with himself. "It proved what I already suspected. Austin is a fraud, so now that the truth is out in the open, there's no longer a reason for you to play coy and pretend that you're unavailable." He slid his fingers down her bare arm. "Now, about your promotion..."

She jerked away from him, gaping incredulously at his nerve. She was tired of battling this man for something she knew she deserved, and she refused to compromise her morals to get it.

And in that moment, she came to a startling realization. This promotion was important to her, yes, but not as much as it once had been. She'd thought she needed to prove to her family that she was self-sufficient, determined and confident, and had put too much emphasis on the senior graphic design position being the direct link to her happiness. Her priorities shifted, and the one topping the list was ultimately pleasing herself—and that meant standing up to this man who believed he wielded so much control over her.

"You know what, Louden? You can take the promotion and shove it," she said matter-of-factly, feeling more unencumbered than she had in years. "And I'm sure the board of directors will find it interesting tomorrow morning to find out exactly how you choose your candidates."

An incensed shade of red traveled up his neck and suffused his face. "It's your word against mine," he said, his tone low and dark with menace.

Grabbing her purse and briefcase, she met his gaze evenly, telling him without words that she wasn't intimidated by him. "I'm willing to take that chance. The last thing I knew, sexual harassment was against the law."

With that parting remark, she started around the opposite side of the desk, her eye on the closed door and her thoughts on quickly escaping this man's hostility. She'd only managed two steps when strong fingers manacled her wrist in a painful grip.

She glared back at Louden, refusing to cower. "Let me go."

A malicious sneer curved his lips. "If you're going to file a complaint, we might as well legitimize it."

And with that, he jerked her around and shoved her against the wall, hard enough that she smacked her head, causing her to lose her grasp on her briefcase and purse, and momentarily paralyzing her entire body. A picture crashed to the floor from the jarring impact, the sound of shattering glass sharp in Teddy's mind.

Stunned and dazed, and trying desperately to gulp air into her lungs, she felt his hands grope at her blouse, then viciously rip it open. Her lips parted to scream, but he clamped a hand over her mouth, nearly smothering her. Refusing to be a victim, she struggled against him as his other hand tugged at the hem of her skirt, then his hand touched her thigh. Swallowing the bile rising in her throat, she shoved against his shoulders, adrenaline lending her a strength she never knew she possessed.

"Oh my God!"

Teddy heard her co-worker's exclamation from somewhere in the office, and it was enough to alarm Louden. He didn't let her go, but instead looked over his shoulder at the intruder. Taking advantage of the distraction, Teddy brought her knee up against his groin, hard. Louden's hands fell away from her to grab himself, and he gaped at her in wide-eyed astonishment. His shock turned to outrage, and though he was in obvious pain, he growled low in his throat and made a last attempt to lunge at her. Her hand shot out to protect herself, and the base of her hand slammed into his nose.

She heard something crack, watched as Louden fell to his knees, clutching both his groin and now-bloody nose. An anguished moan ripped from his chest, and Teddy didn't spare another second to put some distance between them.

On shaking, trembling legs, Teddy managed to round her desk and reach Anna, one of the secretaries in the firm. The woman appeared as shocked as Teddy felt.

"Are you all right?" Anna asked just as two other employees entered her office, obviously having heard the commotion.

"I'm...fine," she assured them all, and with less than steady hands pulled the ends of her blouse back together over her chest. "Someone, call the police, please. I want this man arrested for sexual assault."

12

IT WAS A COLD, cloudy, overcast Saturday afternoon, and neither McBride brother was home, much to Teddy's disappointment. She hadn't called beforehand, afraid that Austin might refuse to see her, and she didn't want to discuss this private matter over the phone.

Sitting on the porch steps leading to the charming old Victorian house that Austin shared with his brother, she waited for over an hour for him to come home, knowing she'd sit there forever if that's how long it took to convince Austin that he was the single-most important thing in her life.

Him, and his love and belief in her.

Coming to that conclusion had been a soul-searching event, but her realization had put so many things into perspective for her. After Louden's attack, she'd spent a few days prioritizing her life, putting her own happiness first on that list, her love for Austin second, and her career third. She no longer felt the need to validate her self-worth to her family, or anyone else, by climbing the corporate ladder. No longer believed that sole independence was the means to ultimate happiness and emotional gratification. She'd put way too much stock in her ambitious goals, when the key to her contentment lay in her heart.

And Austin was in her heart and certainly a part of her soul. She hadn't expected to fall in love with him, never believed a man could make her feel so whole, so emotionally complete. She'd never imagined that the thought of living without him would make her heart ache so unbearably.

Sighing to chase away the nerves fluttering in her stomach, she closed her eyes and leaned back against the stair railing, silently praying that her revelation hadn't come too late.

Fifteen minutes later, his black Mustang turned the corner and drove up the street. Austin glanced out the driver's window, saw her sitting in front of the house, and parked his car in the driveway. Neither brother exited the vehicle, and she could see Austin talking to Jordan, or rather, arguing, if the irritable look on Austin's face was anything to go by.

Finally, Jordan got out of the Mustang, a wide, welcoming smile spreading across his handsome face. "Hi, Teddy," he said, waving her way as he headed toward the front porch. "It's great to see you again."

Austin followed behind at a slower pace, unsmiling, his expression not at all as inviting as Jordan's. Despite his cranky disposition, one that she was no doubt responsible for, he looked absolutely gorgeous in his well-worn jeans and leather jacket, his dark hair tousled so enticingly around his head.

Heart pounding with apprehension, Teddy stood and forced herself to return Jordan's smile. "It's nice to see you again, too, Jordan."

He sauntered casually up the porch stairs, and hooked a finger over his shoulder to indicate Austin. "I'm seriously hoping that you're here to give my brother a much-needed attitude adjustment."

Austin scowled from behind Jordan, but the temperamental gesture was lost on the elder sibling who had way too much mischief glinting in his eyes. "I thought if I sprung for pizza and beer that it might improve his mood, but the man isn't easily swayed by our favorite pastime."

"Jordan," Austin said, his voice vibrating with a low warning.

"Well, it's true," Jordan said as Austin slowly, reluctantly, climbed the stairs to join Jordan and Teddy. "You've been acting like the Grinch since Christmas morning."

Austin's dark green gaze flickered to Teddy, the depths of which were filled with a misery she was all too familiar with. "Maybe that's because someone stole *my* Christmas."

Teddy's heart sank to her knees. What if Austin had decided that he no longer wanted a relationship with her? What if she'd hurt him so badly he no longer trusted her with his love? And what if she'd destroyed the one thing she needed the most from him—the way he believed in her, his unconditional acceptance of who and what she was. She had to make him realize that what she was offering this time wasn't a convenient fling, or a part-time fantasy. It was *the real thing*.

Jordan leaned close, but didn't bother lowering his voice when he spoke. "If my brother is stupid enough to let his pride get in the way of the best thing that's ever happened to him, I'm always available." He gave her a teasing wink, one she suspected was designed to rile his brother.

Jordan's scheme worked. Austin visibly bristled and a possessive light sparked in his eyes. "Get lost, Jordan," he growled fiercely.

A huge, unrepentant grin lifted the corners of Jordan's mouth. "Hey, consider me gone."

Austin stared after his brother with a frown, waiting until Jordan had unlocked the front door and stepped in-

side the house, leaving them well and truly alone. His unfathomable gaze traveled back to her, though he said
nothing, letting the awkward silence stretch between
them.

Since he didn't seem inclined to start any conversation,
she shifted anxiously on her feet and attempted a truce.
"Hi," she said, hating the quiver in her voice.

He didn't offer a polite greeting in return, but cut right
to the chase. "What are you doing here, Teddy?"

"Pleasing myself," she said, the truthful declaration
slipping from her prematurely.

His eyebrows rose, making her realize how selfish that
had sounded, when she'd meant it to be a liberating statement—that she'd finally realized what was important to
her.

"Excuse me?" he asked.

Deciding that starting from the beginning would be the
most logical approach, she drew a calming breath and
said more steadily, "I'm here because I wanted to talk to
you."

He leaned against the opposite railing, folded his arms
over his chest and crossed his legs at his ankles. He offered no verbal encouragement; his seemingly casual
pose the only indication that he was willing to listen to
her.

"I, um, got the promotion," she said, thinking they
could start on neutral territory and work their way to
more personal issues—if he softened up along the way.

"I'm happy for you. I had no doubt you'd get it."

He sounded genuine, and beyond the reservation in his
gaze she caught a glimpse of warmth and sincerity.
Knowing that he still cared gave her hope for what lay
ahead.

As much as she wanted to close the distance between

them, she stayed where she was and forged on, knowing she had to tell him everything, even as unpleasant as some of the recollections were. "Louden was arrested for assault, and I was the one to press charges."

His entire body tensed at that announcement, his expression turning fierce and intense. "What happened?"

She explained the confrontation with Louden in full detail, how he'd assaulted her, how Anna had witnessed the attack, and the fact that Louden spent the night in jail and was fired from Sharper Image. And during her spiel, she watched Austin's body language shift, watched how protective and outraged he became on her behalf. Surprisingly, she found his possessive behavior endearing and chivalrous, not at all smothering.

"Since that incident, three other women in the company have stepped forward with claims of sexual harassment against Louden."

"Good," he said gruffly. "Hopefully, Louden will get his comeuppance."

"Yeah," she agreed. "It looks like he will."

Austin scrubbed a hand along his jaw and released a heavy breath. "So, it sounds like you've got everything you want."

No bitterness coated his words, no resentment, just a resignation that Teddy refused to accept. "Not quite everything," she said quietly, curling her fingers around the top of the railing on either side of her hips. "I want *you.*"

His smile was a little sad. "With that promotion, I doubt you'll have time for me in your life."

She'd given him every reason to express that skepticism, to be leery of her claim. And then she realized that there was one thing left for her to prove after all...her love for Austin.

"You know, the incident with Louden was a real eye-opener," she said, capturing his attention once again.

He frowned at her, though he appeared curious over her statement. "How so?"

"Because it took what happened with Louden to make me realize exactly where my priorities lay." Her fingers gripped the railing tighter, keeping her grounded and focused. "I allowed my narrow-minded goals, and the need for this promotion, to totally consume my life."

His gaze sharpened, turned cautious. "And it no longer matters to you?"

"Oh, it matters," she admitted, knowing she owed him honesty. "But it's not the most important thing in my life anymore. You see, I now have the career I always wanted, but I have no one to share it with." Swallowing the huge knot forming in her chest, she risked everything she had. "And I'm in love with this man who is incredibly generous and understanding and would never do anything to stifle me, but I was too afraid to trust him."

"And he was afraid that he wasn't good enough for you," he replied, his voice a tad rusty.

"What?" she whispered.

"Yeah, it's true." He met her gaze directly, revealing insecurities of his own. "We're so different, you and I. How we were raised, and what we come from. I'm not a blue blood, just a down-to-earth man who doesn't wear a suit unless I absolutely have to. I have no interest in politics, or money, or being an investor, and I own a landscaping business. Most often than not, I come home at night filthy. After meeting your parents, and getting a good idea of what they expect for you, I don't think I would fit in."

She laughed, not because she found his concerns amusing, but because none of those things mattered to her. And judging by the few conversations she'd had with her mother the past two weeks, her parents had warmed to him, too.

"Oh, Austin," she said with a bright smile, one as warm and glowing as their future together. "First of all, I don't give a damn what my parents, or anyone else, thinks about you. *I* love you, just the way you are. But I don't think you have to worry about impressing my mother and father. I get the feeling that they like you. My mother has asked me twice now when I plan to bring you over for dinner again."

"You love me?" he asked, his voice ragged, his gaze filled with pleasure and excitement, and just a hint of disbelief.

"Yeah, I do." Finally closing the distance between them, she wrapped her arms around his neck and pressed her body to his, craving his heat. "And just for the record, Austin, I've never told another man that I loved him," she said, repeating the same words he'd told her Christmas morning. Her feelings for Bart had never extended beyond caring. "You're the first, and I don't make the declaration lightly."

A full-fledged, sexy grin claimed his mouth, and his hands found their way inside her lambskin coat, sliding around to stroke over her jean-clad bottom. "Damn, but you're bossy."

"Yeah, I am, so you'd better get used to it," she said with an impudent smile. Twining her fingers through his thick, soft hair, she brazenly pulled his mouth down to meet hers. "Now shut up and kiss me, because I've missed you so much."

His reply was a deep, thrilling groan that vibrated against her lips. Their time apart dissolved beneath the onslaught of a hot, needy, tongue-tangling kiss. They made magic. They affirmed their love. They both moaned in frustration when the melding of their lips was no longer enough to quench the burning, out-of-control desire that had ignited between them.

"Too many clothes," she complained breathlessly as she stole another deep kiss to assuage her hunger for the taste of him, then slipped her cool hands inside his jacket and beneath his shirt so she could touch his heated flesh. She lost all sense of time and place—she could only think of this man and how he made her feel.

Her entire body tingled, causing her thoughts to shift to more urgent matters. Breaking their kiss, she said huskily, "I want you naked."

His low rumbling laughter tickled her skin as his mouth found the soft hollow under her ear. He nuzzled the sensitive flesh, and she shivered. "I don't think the neighbors would appreciate the public display."

She bit her bottom lip, imagining that sensual mouth on her breasts. Knowing too well the delicious, exquisite sensation of her nipple being finessed by his tongue, she melted a little more. "Should we go back to my place?" she whispered.

He lifted his head, shaking it, his eyes feverish and impatient. "I can't wait that long."

The unmistakable erection pressing against her belly attested to his barely suppressed restraint. Excitement and awareness seized her. "Me neither."

They stared at each other for what seemed like an eternity to Teddy, both of them uncertain as to what to do about this awesome need they had for each other, and how to satisfy it. Then a reckless grin slashed across his features, and she sensed trouble was about to begin. He bent his knees, and in one fluid motion hefted her over his shoulder caveman-style.

A surprised shriek escaped her. By the time she'd

dragged in a breath and could talk again, they were inside
the house, and he was carrying her across the foyer toward a set of stairs that led to the second landing. Blood
rushed to her head, making her dizzy. "Austin!" she said,
choking back laughter, and managing to prop herself up
by bracing her hands on his backside. "Put me down!"

He gave her thigh a loving, intimate squeeze. "In a minute."

Jordan rounded the corner from the living room into
the foyer at that moment, a comical expression on his face
when he saw the two of them. Teddy blushed to the roots
of her hair.

Austin didn't stop his stride. "Don't mind us, Jordan,"
he said, then loped up the stairs, two at a time, giving
Teddy a jarring ride. "We've got an itch that can't wait to
be scratched."

A grin quirked Jordan's mouth, and he reached for the
set of keys on the small table by the front door. "Gotcha.
I'll take this as my cue to 'get lost' again, this time for a
few hours."

"At least," Austin agreed wholeheartedly, shamelessly.
Entering a room, he kicked the door shut behind them,
then lowered her back to her feet.

Light-headed, she swayed slightly, and he grabbed her
hand to steady her. As she gained her balance, Teddy
glanced around, registering the warm, masculine tones of
Austin's room, and the big four-poster antique bed dominating the middle. Her pulse quickened, and she brought
her gaze back to Austin, who was looking at her very intently, their earlier play replaced by something serious
and intimate.

"Will you marry me, Teddy?" he asked, his voice
strong, and clear, and infinitely tender. "If you need time,
I'll give it to you, but I need a commitment."

"You've got it," she assured him, smiling. "I don't need any more time to know that you're the perfect man for me. Yes, I'll marry you."

Relief touched his expression. Framing her face between his palms, he brought her mouth up to his for a kiss that started out gentle and sweet, but quickly escalated into a full-blown seduction. Eager again, she slipped her hands into his jacket and shoved the heavy material off his shoulders and down his arms, letting it fall to the floor. He groaned, and rid her of her coat, too, then lifted her sweater over her head and tossed it aside. Less than five seconds later her bra followed, and he filled his hands with the warm, resilient flesh, rubbed his thumbs over the beaded nipples until her breath caught in her throat.

"Do you mind living here?" he asked, raising his arms so she could peel his shirt off while he toed his loafers off his feet.

She couldn't imagine them living in her small condo when they had such a lovely place to call home. "I'd love to live in your house...and I'd love to have your babies."

That stalled him for a moment, just as he'd unsnapped her jeans and started to unzip them. His gaze jerked to hers, hopeful and searching. "What about your career?"

Giving him a provocative smile, she went to work on his belt buckle. "Weren't you the one who told me I could have it all?" Done with that first task, she took care easing his zipper over the full erection straining the fly of his jeans.

"Yeah, and I'm glad you believe it." He released a tight hiss of breath when her hands slid into his briefs and she took all that hot, hard masculinity into her hands.

Grasping her wrists, he pulled them away from his body and walked her back toward the bed—until the mattress connected with her knees and she was forced to sit.

Then he knelt before her and pulled off her leather boots and socks.

"You'll make a great mom," he said knowingly.

She believed that, too, especially when she had him by her side, supporting her, loving her. He hooked his fingers into the waistband of her jeans, and she lifted her hips so he could pull them off. Then he slowly removed her panties, trailing hot, damp kisses along her belly, her hip, her feminine mound, her quivering thighs...all the way down to her feet.

Dewy and restlessly inflamed, she struggled to keep her mind focused on important issues for just a few minutes longer. "How do you feel about eloping?"

The smoky gaze traveling leisurely, hungrily, up her long legs jumped immediately to her face. "Are you serious? You don't want a big wedding?"

She exaggerated a shudder. "No." She'd been that route before, and didn't need all that pomp and circumstance to pledge her eternal love to Austin.

He raised an eyebrow, and with a tantalizing, calculated roll of his hips that was all for her pleasure, he shimmied out of his own pants. A smile curved her mouth. She planned to extract many more private performances in the future.

"I thought all women wanted a big, fancy wedding," he said, curious and confused.

Anticipation and desire quickened her pulse as she took in his magnificent body. She wriggled back on the bed, until she lay in the center. "I'd strangle my mother before we made it to the ceremony," she said jokingly. "Besides, I want to marry you soon. I don't think I could wait months and months to live with you, and wake up to you every day..."

Grinning in obvious agreement, he moved up onto the

bed, and over her, settling his hips between her welcoming thighs, teasing her with the tip of his shaft. "Is three weeks enough time to make arrangements, and schedule yourself a nice, lengthy vacation?"

"That would be perfect," she murmured, wrapping her legs around his thighs to urge him closer, and drawing his head down so she could kiss him. "But I don't think I can wait another minute for you to make love to me."

"Yes, ma'am," he drawled with a sinful grin, and obliged her, taking her breath away in one smooth, silky thrust of his hips against hers. He touched her heart with his love, filled her soul with that unconditional faith of his, and in the process redefined the word *perfect*.

Epilogue

A MONTH LATER, Teddy and Austin eloped to Waikiki, Hawaii, where they were married by a minister on a bluff overlooking the crystal blue Pacific Ocean. The bride wore a simple cream silk dress complemented with a lei of orchids, and the groom sported dark brown slacks, a cream-colored shirt and an adoring smile as he exchanged wedding vows with the woman who'd stolen his heart.

Afterward, they ordered room service in their bridal suite and sat out on their lanai and fed each other lobster, buttered potatoes and slices of raspberry white-chocolate cheesecake. And when their appetite for food had been appeased, they'd moved to the bedroom and satisfied a more physical and emotional hunger, consummating their love in a ritual as old as time.

Two hours after becoming Mrs. Austin McBride, the only thing Teddy wore was the orchid lei, which Austin had insisted upon, a pink flush on her skin from Austin's loving and the huge rock of a diamond her husband had surprised her with during their wedding ceremony. The ring now replaced the ruby and diamond band she'd worn there for the past year.

Austin propped himself up on his elbow and stared down at his wife, amazed that one woman could make his life so incredibly rich. She looked beautiful, and entirely too pleased with herself. He knew the reason why.

"You do realize, don't you, that your parents are going

to hit the roof when they get your 'wedding announcement' in the mail."

"Yeah." Amusement threaded her husky voice and sparkled in her eyes. She'd asked the minister's wife to take a Polaroid snapshot of the two of them after the ceremony, then on a piece of the hotel's stationery she'd written, "Teddy and Austin announce their wedding to one another," along with the date. She'd sealed both in an envelope, and sent it to her parents in San Francisco so they'd receive the news before Austin and Teddy arrived back home.

She rolled to her back and smiled up at him, looking tousled, and thoroughly satiated. Her breasts were tipped in fragrant orchids, and a few crushed petals clung to her still-damp skin. "I have to admit that it felt good to buck convention."

He laughed. Leave it to Teddy to indulge in one final act of rebellion with her parents. "You sure you're okay with this?"

"Absolutely," she assured him, touching her hand to his jaw. "I couldn't be happier, or more in love, and I don't need a huge ceremony or reception to validate how I feel about you." Then a small frown creased her forehead. "My parents will survive this little catastrophe, though I'm a little worried about Jordan."

"Jordan?" he questioned, wondering what his brother had to do with all that. "Why?"

Her hand absently caressed his chest, and the diamond on her finger caught the light, glittering like a brilliant star. "Well, I know you're trying to sell Fantasy for Hire, but he didn't seem too thrilled about handling the business while you're away."

"He'll be fine." Austin grinned with wry humor. "It's

not as though he's got to worry about fulfilling anyone's fantasy. I only need him to book the dancers."

"I guess you're right, but wouldn't it be great if he found someone like we found each other?" The hopeful quality in Teddy's voice attested to the fondness she seemed to have for Austin's brother. "I mean, I'm sure he's some woman's ideal fantasy."

Austin thought about the possibility of Jordan shedding his conservative image to play some woman's fantasy, but knew his brother would never go for that kind of public performance. Jordan tolerated Fantasy for Hire, but he'd never personally advocate being hired out as someone's fondest desire.

He shook his head at Teddy. "Naw, it'll never happen."

Moving over Teddy, he fitted himself snugly between her thighs, his need for her already fierce and rampant. "Now, what do you say we forget about Jordan, and your parents, and enjoy our honeymoon. I want you, wife."

Smiling a sultry, seductive smile, she lifted the lei of orchids from around her neck and placed it over his head, letting the fragrant flowers fill the air between them. "Consider yourself laid, husband."

HARLEQUIN®

Temptation

There are *Babies...*
Cute! Lovable! A handful!

Then there are **BACHELORS...**
CUTE! SEXY! DEFINITELY A HANDFUL!

What happens when our heroines suddenly
have to deal with *both*?
Find out in the fun new miniseries

BACHELORS & BABIES...

#741 **The Badge and the Baby** Alison Kent (Aug. '99)
#745 **Baby.com** Molly Liholm (Sept. '99)
#749 **The Littlest Stowaway** Gina Wilkins (Oct. '99)
#753 **Oh, Baby!** Leandra Logan (Nov. '99)
#757 **The Good, the Bad and the Cuddly**
Heather MacAllister (Dec. '99)

and more to come!

BACHELORS & BABIES

Available at your favorite retail outlet.

HARLEQUIN®
Makes any time special ™

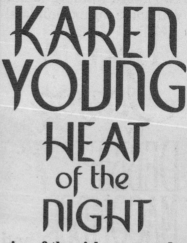

Temptation®

COMING NEXT MONTH

#761 A BABY FOR THE BOSS Jule McBride
Bachelors & Babies

Sexy, macho hostage negotiator Rafe Ransom was forced to undergo sensitivity training by looking after the baby of his assistant McKinley! Soon he found himself bonding with the little boy—and figuring out how to bed the feisty and beautiful mom. Then he learned McKinley had *ulterior* motives....

#762 ALWAYS A HERO Kate Hoffmann
Millennium Book II

Colin Spencer, heir to the Spencer fortune, never knew what hit him. While en route to the party where he'd announce his engagement, he found himself stuck on the elevator with sexy Isabelle Channing and a bottle of bubbly. Next thing he knew, he was a married man. Which wouldn't have been so bad, except that he'd married the wrong woman. Or had he?

#763 BACHELOR BLUES Leanna Wilson

Wade Brooks wasn't looking for everlasting love—but he definitely needed a little female companionship. He wanted someone safe, someone *comfortable*, and Jessie Hart's dating service seemed to be the answer. Only, the sizzling sexual attraction between Wade and the sultry brunette was making Wade decidedly *un*comfortable....

#764 ALL OF ME Patricia Ryan
Blaze

David Waite had been burned once too often by women who pretended to care for him while profiting from his society connections. His solution? "Arm candy"—a beautiful woman to accompany him in public, no strings attached. Nora Armstrong was perfect.... Maybe too perfect, because David found himself wanting to change the rules....

CNM1299

HEART OF THE WEST

Every Man Has His Price!

Lost Springs Ranch was
famous for turning young
mavericks into good men.
So word that the ranch was
in financial trouble sent
a herd of loyal bachelors
stampeding back to
Wyoming to put themselves
on the auction block!